# BEARING TWO THREE ZERO

Andy Jones

www.ajonesauthor.com

ISBN: 978-1-0369-2882-7

Also by Andy Jones

*Call Sign Panther*

With thanks to Rob, Sue, Liz, Ant, David and Jemma

# Chapter 1

## Rhubarb

February 1941 Northern France.

Filthy grey cloud obscured my view and sent beads of moisture racing over the canopy. It was an awful day for flying, but the bad weather was hiding us as we pushed on into enemy territory. We had crossed the French coast at the Pas De Calais and then flown a dog leg course into the Somme Valley, here we had turned north. I had carefully planned this convoluted route so we could hit the target without being detected … hopefully.

Every now and then, through gaps in the cloud, I'd catch a glimpse of the stark winter scenery below. I felt snug and secure in the cockpit of the Spitfire and yet only a thin skin of metal protected me against the hostile world outside. I twisted my shoulder against the straps and glanced over the port quarter. Gilroy was still there, holding formation about fifty feet behind me. I checked my watch. We had been flying on the same bearing for two minutes, which meant we had covered ten miles. I reached forward and clicked the transmit button on the radio to speak.

"Osprey two, descending now."

"Roger Osprey leader." I heard Gilroy's distorted voice through my headphones.

I pushed the nose down and to compensate for the increase in speed I throttled the engine back. We broke through the cloud and dropped low into the valley. Below us the river snaked its way north. The banks were lined by rows of naked trees, beyond which the fields and meadows were flooded. The landscape looked dank and miserable.

I glanced at the compass. The little black instrument with its thin white line gave a bearing of three-hundred and twenty-five degrees, we were still on track. Through the misty drizzle I could just make out some buildings on the horizon. In the centre was a tall grey tower, the Church of Saint-Vulfran. This imposing gothic structure, which sat in the centre of Abbeville, was the landmark I'd been looking for.

"Osprey two, I've got the town and steeple at two o'clock," I called over the radio.

"Roger Osprey leader."

I turned gently to starboard and headed towards the church. We raced over the town, the tiled rooftops passing just beneath our wings. Flying at three hundred miles an hour just above the ground was exhilarating. There was no margin for error. A small misfire from the engine or slight misjudgement from the pilot could be disastrous. Looking ahead I could see the road which ran towards an airfield, this was our target. I called over to Gilroy.

"Osprey two, I'm starting my attack."

"Understood Osprey leader, I'm breaking off now."

The airfield was positioned about two miles north of the town. It had been occupied by the Luftwaffe when the German army invaded France. During the winter some of their squadrons had been pulled back from the area, but our intelligence suggested it was now being used as a forward operating base for fighters. Our brief was to attack the airfield and inflict as much damage as possible.

That morning Gilroy and I had spent time studying maps of the area and had devised a plan. Once we reached the town centre I would climb to about a thousand feet and then dive into my attack, running across the airfield from south to north. At the same time, Gilroy would break to port and then take a long sweeping turn into his attack run from west to east, immediately after mine. We would then regroup and head home over the Channel as quickly as possible. So far everything was going to plan. Even in the appalling weather we had kept on course by watching our speed and checking our bearings.

I pulled back on the stick and climbed steeply. Almost at once I was back up in the thick cloud which meant I had to push forward into a dive sooner than I had hoped. My eyes followed the road, at the end of which I could see an area of flat ground bisected by a long strip of short grass - the airfield and runway.

In front and below was a small aircraft hangar with an apex roof. I banked slightly to bring the building square into my gunsight. I was about a quarter of a mile away and rapidly closing on it. I slid my thumb over the brass fire button and squeezed. All eight of my machine guns rattled into life. I saw small puffs of chalk and gravel fly up around the base of the building as my bullets hammered home. I kept firing until I was a mere hundred feet above the ground. Then I let go of the button and pulled the stick hard back. I skimmed over the tin roof with what felt like a few inches of clearance. I was satisfied I'd hit the target, but instantly knew that something was wrong. I'd expected to see more than just one building and some signs of activity. In fact, the whole airfield seemed too quiet.

I looked over my starboard wing and immediately realised my mistake. Over to the east were three large hangars, much bigger than the building I'd just shot up. Parked outside were several aircraft. I'd misjudged my position and flown straight past the main target.

By now I was over the centre of the airfield. I was too low to turn and attempt an attack on the other buildings. I also knew that Gilroy would now be coming in from the left hand side and there was a danger we might collide. My only choice was to fly straight, climb up and then sweep into the attack again. I was furious with myself and cursed loudly.

Just then something bright flickered ahead. I peered over the nose and saw the orange muzzle flash of an anti-aircraft gun. We had expected some flak, but I was surprised to see at least three twenty-millimetre cannons were positioned directly in front of me. To climb now would be fatal, I would slow down and present myself as an easy target. I had to keep the Spitfire straight and level and hammer on as fast as I could past the guns.

I saw more muzzle flashes, but I was over and gone

before they could draw a bead on me. Once clear I turned to port and gently climbed. As I looked back over the airfield I could see Gilroy coming in from the west on his attack run. From my position I had a perfect view of the tragedy as it unfolded. I had been lucky, the guns weren't ready for me and by flying directly towards them I'd been a difficult target to hit. Now they were awake and Gilroy was flying across them at a right angle.

I watched helplessly as the guns opened up on him. He had managed to cover half the distance of the airfield before I saw a puff of white smoke come up from his engine and a jagged chunk of metal fly from the fuselage. He had been flying very low, maybe only fifty feet from the ground. His port wing dropped and the tip skimmed the grass. For a brief moment he looked as if he might get the aircraft back straight and level, but then the tip dug back into the ground and the aircraft cartwheeled nose over tail into a small copse of trees. A great orange flame crowned by a mushroom of black smoke rose up instantly. Christ!

I flicked my wings over, turned away from the airfield and instantly discarded any thoughts of continuing my attack. Those guns would be looking for me now and every enemy fighter in the area would be alerted to my presence.

Our plan had been that after the attack we would take a course directly northwest, as it was the quickest route to the English Channel. I dived back down into the valley and headed off flying as low as I could. All the while I scanned the skyline for any dangers such as tall trees, telegraph cables and powerlines. At one point the terrain either side of me rose up and I found myself flying level with the houses on the hillside. Every now and then I would weave to the side, just in case a fighter had crept up behind me, but at that speed and altitude I doubted anything could catch me.

The weather towards the coast was getting worse. A thick pallid band of mist obscured the horizon. Then suddenly the earth below fell flat and the brown fields gave way to the yellow sandy beach of Saint Quentin. Beyond the shoreline I could see the turbulent waves of the English Channel. I kept low and as I crossed the sand dunes I saw a solitary figure standing on the beach. Around his feet an excited dog was charging back and forth. The man stood watching me with his hands tucked into his pockets. I wondered who he was. A French villager out for a stroll or maybe a German officer about to report my position? As soon as I was over the sea I pulled up hard into the cloud. As I did I checked my watch: fourteen-twenty-six.

The world outside my cockpit turned into a brilliant white. There was comfort in being hidden by the cloud. Here I was safe from being attacked, but there were other dangers. Having no visual reference of the horizon could be disorienting and it was easy to stall or spin the aircraft. I kept a careful watch on the instruments in front of me, checking that my rate of climb was not too great and my speed was fast enough.

The needles on the altimeter spun clockwise past the painted digits on the dial. At three thousand feet the cloud thinned, then a dazzling ray of golden sunshine cut through the vapour and made me squint. I was above the cloud in a clear atmosphere. I held the aircraft steady and then using the small wheel by my left leg trimmed the Spitfire for level flight.

From the top of my right flying boot I pulled out a folded map and after some rummaging found a thick pencil. I turned the map over until I found the section which showed the Channel between the Pas de Calais and the Sussex shoreline. Marked on the map were some notes I'd made when we'd planned the operation. I had calculated that the distance between both coasts was fifty-nine miles. That meant I should be over Hastings in around twelve minutes. I pushed the map and pencil back into the top of my boot. I quickly checked my bearing and then cast an eye over the engine oil pressure and radiator temperature. It was running a little hot, but that wasn't surprising. Underneath my flying jacket and jumper my shirt was saturated with sweat. I shivered as my body started to relax and the cold, wet material stuck to my back.

This was the sixth offensive sweep that I had carried out in the last month. Twice we had been called back at the last moment; twice we had failed to find the target. Apart from today we had only carried out one successful attack.

The German army now occupied most of mainland Europe. During the spring and early summer of 1940, they had invaded the Netherlands, Belgium and France. Then they set their sights on Britain, but to successfully cross the English Channel meant having air supremacy and then suppressing the Royal Navy. It was an ambitious plan and at one point they seemed deadly serious about attempting it. Their first task was to destroy the Royal Air Force. What followed was a gruelling air battle which raged on for four months over the summer.

I had joined my first squadron at the beginning of the conflict. We were flying Hawker Hurricanes from an airfield north of London. It was a vicious baptism of fire for a young twenty-year-old. I had been incredibly lucky, I'd escaped a number of close shaves and even managed to claim a few enemy aircraft. But at the height of the battle, I was forced to bail out and in doing so badly injured my arm which put me out of action for several weeks. By then the Luftwaffe's offensive had slackened off and the threat of invasion drifted away. In the late autumn I was posted to a squadron based at RAF Manston on the east coast of Kent. I had to spend some time learning to fly Spitfires and eventually returned to operational duties in early December. We flew defensive patrols most days and were occasionally scrambled to intercept the odd bomber, but it appeared the enemy's tactics had changed and they now favoured raiding us by night.

It had been a strange Christmas, it was the first I'd spent away from my family. I found it novel to spend the day lazing around the squadron crew room rather than attending church and opening presents. In the Officers' Mess we were served chicken and a 'mock' Christmas pudding stuffed with dried fruit and breadcrumbs. Despite the food rationing we drank heavily, and Boxing Day was spent in the blur of a hellish hangover.

In the New Year we had been ordered to carry out a series of low level attacks over Northern France. These operations were known by the code name Rhubarb. The idea was to pick a potential target such as an airfield, fuel depot or train yard and swoop in for a surprise attack. At first we had flown in large formations, but recently we had been trying smaller groups and pairs of aircraft.

We were asked, or rather encouraged, to volunteer for these operations. At first I was very keen, it was an opportunity to take the fight back across the Channel and after weeks of inactivity I had begun to get frustrated. I always enjoyed the challenge of navigation and found the flying exciting, but the results weren't paying the dividends we'd expected. Today's operation had been a prime example; one pilot and aircraft lost and all I'd managed to do was put a handful of bullets into an empty tin shed.

At fourteen-thirty-eight I judged I was a few miles from the coast. I was still being suffocated by the bad weather and at that altitude I had no way of visually confirming my position. I checked the fuel gauges by my knee. Flying low and fast had burnt more fuel than I'd expected - I had thirty gallons to get me home.

I eased the throttle back, dropped into the cloud and the world went white again. My plan was to descend and pick up a landmark, but the cloud was thicker than I'd hoped. I carefully watched the numbers on the altimeter which were now spinning anticlockwise. Then, below me where I expected to see land, was the grey spume of the Channel. I levelled off just under the cloud base and tried to assess my position. I was now surrounded by a curtain of rain and visibility was very bad.

Where on earth was I? I was convinced that I'd flown the correct bearing and had to assume there had been a terrific head wind which had slowed me down. I pulled out the map again and checked my calculations; they all seemed correct. I looked up and strained my eyes through the canopy. I had an uneasy feeling looking over the featureless grey gloom that stretched out below. My shoulders stiffened with tension, I didn't have enough fuel to be messing around. At length I spotted a thin dark line in the distance. It was the Sussex coast. According to my plots on the map I judged I was approaching the town of Hastings. Somehow I'd either miscalculated the distance or my speed, but whatever error had been made it didn't matter now. I breathed a sigh of relief as I crossed the coast and turned northeast.

The landscape appeared flatter than I remembered. I'd spent a few holidays in Hastings and I knew that to the east of the town a cliff rose up about two hundred feet high. The geography seemed to be wrong, but in the bad visibility it was hard to tell. I scanned the area for any other form of landmark, but could see nothing, I was lost. With such bad weather and my fuel running low, I reluctantly decided to use the radio and ask for help.

Before the outbreak of war, England had been covered in radio detection transmitters. These were able to detect and track aircraft as part of the air defence system. Primarily this was to safeguard against enemy intruders, but they could also be used as navigational aids. The idea was that a friendly aircraft transmitted a radio signal, this was picked up by the stations on the ground, who then triangulated the position and let the pilot know roughly where he was. They were often used by bomber crews coming back from long range raids. Fighter pilots, like myself, were less likely to need them as we tended to operate during the day and in good visibility. As useful as the system was, being forced to ask for help with my navigation was a blow to my professional pride. However, my situation was not getting any better and a smashed up aircraft would be a greater bruise to my ego. I pressed the transmit button on the radio set.

"Hello, Osprey leader here, can anyone hear me?"

After a moment of silence a voice crackled back through my headphones.

"Osprey leader, this is Beetle, go ahead."

Beetle? That was the call sign for Tangmere which was a good fifty miles away from where I should be.

"Hello Beetle, can you give me a fix please?"

"Yes, can you ensure you're transmitting on the correct frequency?" I checked the dial on the controller unit and then waited patiently, while on the ground teams of radio operators hidden away in wooden huts plotted my position. I pulled out the map once more and prepared for the response.

"Osprey this is Beetle. We have you just north of Shoreham." That was not what I was expecting. I must have been a good five degrees off course when I crossed the Channel. The radio crackled again.

"Osprey, what is your destination? The weather has closed in across the south and has affected all local airfields."

"Hello Beetle, I'm heading to Manston." There was a pause.

"The controller suggests you try and get down as soon as

possible." It was a sensible suggestion, but I was keen to get home. According to the map, I was further away from where I wanted to be, but maybe I could make it back on the fuel I had.

"Thank you Beetle, I'll try and push on."

"Okay Osprey, understood. Good luck." There was a hint of sarcasm in the operator's voice.

All around me the sky was still grey and miserable, but towards the north it seemed slightly brighter. I thought that maybe over the Downs where the ground was higher the weather might be better. I turned and headed towards a small patch of white cloud ahead.

I'd covered about twenty miles when the weather improved slightly, but beyond in the distance it looked like it was getting worse again. Just then I noticed a peculiar rotund building about a mile away to the east below me. This odd futuristic construction contrasted oddly against the countryside. Running from the building, two long concrete roadways led to a flat grass area. I'd seen the building before and had some notion it was a civilian aerodrome.

I checked the fuel tank gauge again. The needle told me I had less than ten gallons left. My options were running out and I needed to get down on the ground. This aerodrome looked like my best bet.

I eased the wing over and flew around in a wide circuit. I could see three large hangars at the far end and outside of these a few aircraft were parked. I noticed the words British Airways Limited painted in huge black letters on the side of one of the hangars. I couldn't see any other aircraft moving either on the ground or in the air, but then again who would have been that stupid to fly in those conditions?

Satisfied that it all looked safe I decided to wake everybody with a low pass before coming into land. I dropped the nose and aimed directly at the rotunda. I passed overhead at no more than two hundred feet. If anyone was around they'd know I was attempting to land. I climbed slightly and turned into the downwind circuit. I throttled right back then reached up and slid the canopy open so I was exposed to the elements. I pushed the undercarriage lever down and listened to the hydraulics whirring. Two dull thuds and three green lights on the instrument panel told me I had wheels to land on. I looked back at the airfield, it was a long runway and I reckoned I had plenty of space to get down safely. Banking the wing and using a little rudder I slipped into the final approach, all the while losing height. I bumped down onto the grass at the western end of the airfield and let the aircraft rumble over the ground. As I slowed down, the cold rain which had been forced over the canopy by the rush of air now started to infiltrate the cockpit and hit my face.

Taxiing a Spitfire is hard work. With the tail on the ground and the engine cowling rising up in front, it is impossible to see directly forward of the cockpit. To make matters worse I had no idea where I was supposed to be heading, but thought it best to head in the direction of the hangars. Out of the misty rain I saw a grey vehicle heading towards me. It pulled over to the side of the runway and a man in dark blue overalls jumped out. I slowed to a stop and he ran over to my wingtip. He waved his right hand frantically in the direction he wanted me to go. I let go of the brake and started moving again with the man alongside me. I was grateful for his presence, as he shepherded me safely onto the concrete apron and signalled me to park outside one of the hangars. By the time we had stopped I was saturated. A small pool of water had formed in my lap and soaked through my uniform. I cut the switches and the drone of the engine, which had kept me company for the past two hours, was replaced with the heavy patter of rain. The man in overalls ran up to me and I saw a pair of corporal's chevrons on his arm. I looked down at him from the cockpit.

"Where the bloody hell am I?" I barked. I was frustrated at my navigational mistake and didn't like being lost.

"This is Gatwick, RAF Gatwick - sir." The name meant nothing to me.

"What's the nearest town?"

"We're about two miles north of Crawley." I pulled the map out of my boot. The corporal jumped up on the wing and leant into the cockpit. With a grubby forefinger he pointed out our position on the map. I was very far from where I wanted to be, but I was down and safe.

"Can you get this refuelled and rearmed?" I asked him as I undid my straps and unplugged my headset.

"We can give you some juice, but I don't think we've got any ammunition. I'm afraid we're not an active station sir."

"Which squadrons are based here?"

"There's an army co-operation unit and some civilians." I stood up on the seat and climbed out of the cockpit. After two hours of flying my body was stiff and tense. It felt good to be out of the aircraft but the cold rain and sharp wind were very unpleasant.

"Where's the ops room? I'd better report in." I asked as I slid the cockpit cover shut.

"The big round building over there, they call it the Beehive. I'll run you over."

With that the corporal jogged back to pick up the van that he had abandoned on the side of the runway. I took the opportunity to walk around the Spitfire and make sure I hadn't taken any damage. The machine was practically brand new, but it looked well used. The fuselage was streaked with dirty oil stains, mud was splattered over the wheels and undercarriage. The paint on the leading edges of the wings had been worn away, the result of flying through heavy rain at three hundred miles an hour.

The corporal dropped me outside the main entrance to the Beehive, this was the building I'd seen from the air. It was a strange circular structure made of cast concrete and painted white. The corporal told me it had been built as an airport terminal which allowed passengers direct undercover access to the aircraft. The main door was flanked by two pillars of sandbags and in the centre stood a guard. Rainwater was dripping from the rim of his tin helmet onto his khaki green cape. A Lee Enfield rifle rested against his left shoulder. As I approached he came to attention.

"Can I see your pass, sir?" he asked officiously.

"No, I haven't got one." It was a strict rule that when flying over enemy territory you emptied your pockets of any papers or information. All I was carrying was my flying helmet, a soggy map and a pound note. "I've just landed and I need to report into the ops room."

"I'm afraid no one can enter without a pass, sir."

"That's my Spitfire over there," I pointed over towards the hangar. "Do I look like a German spy?"

"Well, I can't tell, you might be one." I glared at him. He raised his shoulders and shifted the weight on his feet. "I have my orders sir. I can't let anyone in without the correct pass."

"Then, if that's the case go and tell someone inside that I've just landed."

"Can't do that sir. I'm not allowed to leave my post."

"Look, I haven't got the patience for this. Knock on the ruddy door, get someone out." With that I stepped forward, he moved to the side blocking my way.

"I'm sorry sir if you've not got a pass, I can't help you."

"For heaven's sake!" I raised my voice. "I've just flown over the Channel through two hours of shitty weather and a flak barrage. I'm soaking bloody wet and getting wetter. I need to report back to my squadron. Either let me in or knock on the door!"

Just then the door opened and a tall lean officer stepped outside.

"What's all this about?" He asked sternly. The guard snapped back to attention.

"This man is trying to gain access to the operations room and he hasn't got a pass. Sir." The officer looked me up and down.

"Good lord, … Jack?" He said with a smile. I recognised his thin red hair and Celtic eyes, his name was Fraser. We'd learnt to fly together at the same airfield over a year before.

He stepped forward into the rain, pushed past the guard and shook my hand.

"What the hell are you doing here?"

"I was out of fuel, so I had to land somewhere." I nodded towards where the Spitfire was parked.

"Oh, it was you that came in just now. We wondered what all the noise was about. Were you out patrolling on your own?"

"I've just come back over the Channel. There were two of us, but I left my wingman in France."

"Blimey! Are you okay?"

"I think so, apart from getting soaked in this rain."

"Where were you heading back to?"

"Manston, but I couldn't see a bloody thing and drifted off course over the Channel." I reluctantly accepted that my navigation had failed.

"The weather's closed in right the way across the south. They don't reckon it'll clear for a while." Fraser flicked his arm up and looked at his watch. "It'll be dark in an hour, looks like you'll be staying the night." I looked up at the bleak sky and sighed.

"Get yourself over to the mess and book in. We can grab a bite to eat and maybe a drink later. I'll make sure your kite gets refuelled, they can stick it in the hangar overnight."

He gave me directions and I trudged over to the Officer's Mess. Here I managed to get a call back to Manston to tell them I was safe, but that Gilroy had been lost. It was strange reporting Gilroy's death down a telephone line. It seems so matter of fact. I knew he was dead, but they wouldn't be able to officially confirm it. For now he would be posted as 'missing in action'. I put the receiver down knowing that a telegram was already being prepared for his next of kin. In the last year I'd lost a lot of friends and although my emotional resilience had toughened, each death left a scar.

To my delight I found that the Mess had good hot showers which I took advantage of while my wet clothes dried in front of a stove. Fraser joined me at dinner.

"So, what have you been up to?" He asked as the mess steward served us two small lamb chops.

"I was posted on to Hurricanes after the course. Arrived at North Weald last July."

"My God, you must have been in the thick of the battle."

"Oh yes, six weeks of hell." I helped myself to some potatoes.

"I heard you got the DFM." Fraser nodded towards the medal ribbon I wore on my chest. "You had some good action then?"

"A fair bit, but I was lucky. What about you, I thought you were going on to Coastal Command?"

"Aye, a big mistake though. It was fairly dull work. I did get a couple of long trips down to Gibraltar, those were fun. But after a while I got fed up with staring at the sea so I applied for a posting. They sent me on a conversion course and I wound up here as an Army Co-Op pilot."

A series of army co-operation squadrons had been established with the aim of providing ground support to the army. Their duties included artillery spotting, battlefield communications and air to ground fire support. The aircraft they were equipped with tended to be slow and the nature of the work had never appealed to me. I preferred the freedom and speed a fighter pilot had.

"What are you flying?" I asked.

"Westland Lysanders."

"Any good?"

"Aye, brilliant aircraft. All the strength of a biplane and still reasonably fast."

"What are they like in the air?"

"Masses of lift and you can land it on a billiard table, but it takes a little getting used to. It has these flaps and slats which deploy automatically and can catch you out." Fraser rested his cutlery and reached for a jug of water.

"What happened on your trip today?" He offered me a glass. I stared at the clear liquid, I was beginning to hanker for something stronger.

"It was a bloody shambles," I grumbled. "The trouble is the aircraft is not up to it."

"You surprise me, I've heard good things about the Spitfire."

"It's not the performance, it's just not the right tool for the job. As good as the Spitfire is, by the time you find the target you've got limited ammunition to do any damage. If you're really going to smash a place up you need bombs, but then with the extra weight you wouldn't have the speed or the range. They keep promising us better armament, but we've not seen anything yet. These jobs are best left to the bomber boys, but the powers that be keep sending us over."

It was hard to sleep that night. The image of Gilroy's

aircraft exploding played over in my mind and somehow merged with all the other aircraft I'd seen crash and burn. I hated the sober darkness and the terrors it brought. Eventually, I gave in to my full bladder and navigated my way down the dark corridor to find the facilities. As I returned to my room I heard the distant sound of an engine starting. It surprised me that anyone would be running an engine up at that time of night so I walked over to the window and curiously drew back the heavy black out curtain.

The sky was clearer now and the moonlight cast an eerie shimmer across the airfield. In the shadows I could just make out the shape of an aircraft with a lick of flame lashing from its exhaust. It trundled out slowly towards the runway. I lost sight of it as it disappeared into the shadows, but I could still hear the engine. Suddenly I saw it lift into the sky, its wide wing catching the moonlight.

So, this was one of the Lysanders that Fraser had mentioned. It was a strange looking bird with a plump fuselage and large radial engine. It was equipped with a bulky fixed undercarriage that hung down like a pair of workman's boots. The cantilever wing, which was attached above the canopy, had a very distinctive shape that tapered towards the root like the wing of a dragonfly. I knew that the Lysander had been designed as a battlefield support aircraft but was pretty much obsolete by the outbreak of war. I'd heard rumours that they were now being used for covert night operations, ferrying spies in and out of enemy territory. With its short take off and landing it was ideal for such work.

The thought of an operation like that terrified me and yet strangely I was happy to cross the Channel and attack whatever I found. The difference was as a pilot, just like a soldier or sailor, there was mutual honour and respect between adversaries. If I was to be shot down and captured there were treaties that protected me. However, a spy didn't have that luxury; if they were caught they most probably would be tortured and then executed. I wondered if that courtesy would be extended to the pilot of the aircraft bringing them in. It was dangerous and important work for little personal reward. I watched as the aircraft turned away from the airfield and disappeared into the darkness.

The next morning the weather was clear enough for me to travel home. I was keen to get going, so immediately after breakfast Fraser took me over to the hangar where my aircraft was parked. I took off and then in customary style flew back over the hangars, waggling my wings in a farewell gesture.

# Chapter 2

## Manston

The sky was still overcast, but flying was considerably easier than the day before. I flew a direct course back across the Kent countryside and reached Manston in less than twenty minutes. The airfield was situated just inland from the seaside town of Ramsgate, about seventy miles southeast of London. Manston had been operating as a military airfield since the First World War. Being just thirty miles from the French coast it was strategically important to the defence of the country. The previous summer it had been a key target for the Luftwaffe, who had attacked the airfield relentlessly. On one day alone, twenty-nine people were killed and the airfield was all but destroyed. The scars of that tragic summer were still visible, bomb craters, broken windows and piles of rubble were everywhere you walked.

I touched down and taxied up to the apron, being careful to avoid several vast patches of waterlogged grass. Two of the ground crew greeted me in their heavy rubber boots and thick overcoats. The ground crew were officially designated as Aircraftsmen, but over time the name had been shortened and they were affectionately known as 'erks'.

"Morning sir," said one of them as I climbed out of the cockpit. "Good to see you made it back. Any damage to report?"

I looked back at the aircraft remembering the flak cannons that had been firing at me over Abbeville.

"No, I don't think so." I took off my leather flying helmet and smoothed my hair back into place. "But please give her a good look over, will you?"

I squelched over the soft ground towards the squadron crew room. It was one of several large wooden huts which had been constructed to replace the buildings destroyed in the bombing.

All around soil had been banked up to form blast pens, semicircular mounds that were wide enough for an aircraft to be parked inside and designed to offer some protection against air raids. The earthworks, along with the bomb craters, had ruined the drainage system meaning the ground outside the crew room was always wet. Within a month of constant use, it had become impossible to enter or exit the building without wading through mud. The hut had been hastily erected, one of the windows was missing its glass and, in an effort to stop a howling gale ripping through the building, the bottom of an old tea chest had been nailed over the aperture.

As I carefully negotiated my way over a wooden plank, I passed two men. One was a civilian workman in a woollen jacket and flat cap, the other I judged to be some sort of official wearing a long trench coat and trilby. They were arguing over where a roadway was to be laid down.

"The plans quite clearly show the concrete coming up to this boundary here." The official pointed to a piece of folded paper he held in his hand.

"My gaffer has sent the roller back to the yard. We can't flatten this lot by hand," complained the man in the flat cap.

The squadron was at readiness and inside I found the duty pilots sitting around waiting for orders. Although, in this weather it was highly unlikely any enemy aircraft would appear. One sergeant pilot was asleep in a wicker chair, two others were reading books and in the corner an intense chess game was taking place. On the wall a large blackboard listed the names of all the available pilots. In the blank space below mine Gilroy's name was faintly visible. I dropped my helmet onto an armchair and took off my flying gloves.

"You made it back then." Mundy, another Pilot Officer like myself, was sitting with his feet up on a table.

"Just about … Gilroy didn't make it."

"So I heard."

"Is that today's?" I pointed to a newspaper resting in his lap.

"Yes, not much going on though." He threw the paper across to me. "Usual tripe, Churchill's trying to convince the Americans to help us out. There's a good piece on Olivia De Haviland with a few pictures."

I opened out the paper and looked at the front page, there was not much of interest to me. I glanced over an article that speculated about what would be Hitler's next big play. Some people suggested the Mediterranean and North Africa, others said Russia. However, it meant little to us pilots twiddling our thumbs in the middle of a quagmire. Apart from the low-level raids, we had not been very active and after the incredible excitement of the previous summer's battle, I'd found the last two months somewhat anticlimactic. I lit a cigarette and offered one to Mundy, he bent forward to take a light from my match.

"By the way, the old man wants to see you." By this he meant our Commanding Officer. The news didn't surprise me. I'd have to record what had happened the day before in a formal report.

"Where is he?"

"He's over in his lair."

I left via the backdoor, where it was less muddy, and crossed over towards another hut which served as the Squadron Headquarters. I entered the outer office where a female clerk sat typing briskly and a sergeant was scratching his head over a volume of King's Regulations; neither of them noticed me. I took a final drag on the cigarette and stubbed it into an ashtray on the clerk's desk. Her fingers paused for a moment as she looked up at me. I smiled, she twisted her lip and resumed her typing. I turned around and knocked on the door to the inner office.

"Yes!" came a surly voice from the other side. As I opened the door I was hit by a blast of warm air. In the corner of the office a large pot-belly stove was glowing orange. A dim light filtered through the windows that were fogged with condensation. Sitting sideways behind an oak desk and reading a letter was George Campbell, my Commanding Officer. He was a big man who appeared to be out of proportion with the rest of the room. Campbell was immensely proud to be Scottish and yet he'd spent his entire life in Rhodesia, hated the cold and didn't have the slightest whisp of a Scot's brogue.

"Where the hell did you end up?" he asked curtly as I entered.

"Gatwick," I replied, "The only place I could get down in that weather."

"Gatwick? Where on earth is that?"

"Sussex."

"You got lost then?"

"Not sure, I thought the compass might have been out, but more likely I was blown off course over the Channel." I felt like adding that I was also distracted by the battery of German gunners trying to shoot me down, but Campbell was not a man to be sarcastic with.

"Did you get hit?"

"Not that I know of, but the erks are looking over the aircraft now." I shifted the weight on my feet.

"Sit down, for god's sake." He gestured at a wooden chair and then shouted into the outer office. "Crouch!" The young clerk came to the door.

"Take this shit away. I can't drink it." Campbell pushed a coffee cup towards the edge of the desk.

"Sorry sir, would you like a fresh cup?"

"Not unless you've got a stock of fresh Kenyan coffee beans in that desk of yours."

"Afraid not sir, only powdered substitute."

"I'd rather go thirsty." Campbell muttered as Crouch picked up the cup and left the room.

"So, what happened yesterday then?" he turned back

towards me.

"Everything went according to plan until we hit the airfield. We took them by surprise, but they had at least two flak batteries there." I wanted to be clear that Gilroy's death wasn't my fault.

"Did you manage to hit anything?"

"Difficult to say, I only had a chance to make one pass."

"Not a great show then." There was a condescending tone to his questioning. I felt I needed to justify myself.

"Intelligence said there would be little or no defence around the airfield and the Met boys said the cloud base would lift before we got there." Campbell raised an eyebrow.

"The weather should have been to your advantage."

"Not when the cloud is that low. Soon as I climbed to start my attack I couldn't see the damn target."

Campbell threw down the letter he was reading and stared at me with a pair of fierce dark eyes. I'd overstepped the mark and by the look of things was about to suffer the consequences. Fortunately, my punishment was postponed as just then the door behind me opened softly and the Station Commander, Group Captain Willington entered. I quickly rose to my feet, Campbell slowly got to his, but before he reached the full extent of his six feet three inches Willington spoke.

"Good morning gentlemen, as you were, please." He waved his hands and took the chair alongside mine. Willington, like Campbell, was also tall, but his frame was much thinner and his face was almost gaunt.

"I'm just doing the rounds," he had a thin voice with

very precise diction. "Any luck yesterday?" He looked over at me. As the Station Commander he oversaw the day to day running of the airfield and had an eye on all the planned operations.

"We lost an aircraft and pilot, I can't say it was a great success sir."

"Thank you Sommers, I'll give the briefings here." Campbell interrupted me sharply.

"The target was Abbeville, wasn't it?" enquired Willington.

"Yes, the airfield just north of the town." Campbell answered for me.

"I know that area well. Many memories." Willington smiled, he was a veteran of the First World War and had obviously spent time in that region of France. "And we lost a pilot?"

"Unfortunately so. It appears they've reinforced the defences around the area." Once again, Campbell answered for me.

"That's interesting, I wonder why they've done that?" Willington mused. "I'm sure the intelligence chaps will be keen to know what you saw."

Was that one pathetically small piece of information worth a man's life, I thought. Willington looked at me and seemed to read my mind.

"Don't worry Sommers. These operations aren't in vain. Every time we send an aircraft over the Channel it keeps Jerry on his toes. Remember you're taking the fight to him," he said jovially.

"With all due respect sir, flying over there with just a

handful of bullets hardly seems worth it." There was a limit to how long I could bite my lip. Willington's face drooped into a frown and revealed his age.

"It doesn't matter what you hit or what damage you do." His voice became stern. "The strategy is to keep harassing the enemy so he's forced to play his cards early." He stood up, Campbell and I followed suit. "On another matter," Willington spoke directly to Campbell. "The Air Vice Marshall is due to visit us on Thursday, please make yourself available." As he walked towards the door he stopped and looked at me. "Make sure you put on a good show." He left the office leaving the door open. Campbell was glaring at me, his face burning brighter than the pot belly stove.

"Shut the door," he snarled with both fists clenched on the desk. I took a step backwards and closed the door. "I don't want any of that talk around here," he growled. "It's not your job to work out strategy and the last thing I need is any dissention in the ranks." He threw himself back down into his chair. "And just because you've got that medal pinned to your chest doesn't give you licence to shoot your mouth off."

Although he was senior to me and more experienced, Campbell's chest was bare and his logbook only claimed half an enemy aircraft whereas I had five in mine. This was all pure luck and no reflection on his abilities as a pilot. During the Battle of Britain he had been posted to a remote airfield in Wales far from the frontline, while I had been sent to a squadron stationed in the thick of the fighting. Ever since I'd arrived at Manston he'd harboured a resentment towards me. Although this didn't bother me at first, over the last few weeks I noticed my patience had become thinner and my tongue had become sharper.

Campbell reached across his desk and picked up a yellow slip of paper, he waved it at me.

"I've had a memo from Group. They're asking for volunteers. Ideally pilots with combat experience and more than ten hours flying on Spitfires." He pointed at me. "You fit the bill so I'm volunteering you."

"Do I have a choice in the matter, sir?"

"Certainly not," he sniffed.

"Can I ask what I'm volunteering for?"

"I haven't a clue, it doesn't say." Campbell flicked the memo over to see if anything was written on the back. "It just says report to Heston Airfield this coming Monday."

I knew Heston, it was like Gatwick, a civilian airfield to the west of London, there were no fighters stationed there. My heart sank, maybe I had pushed it too far this time and Campbell had cunningly stitched me up with a dead end job ferrying biplanes for the rest of the war.

# Chapter 3

## Greatcoat

The little yellow slip of paper ordered me to report to 'Number 2 Camouflage Unit, Heston Airfield' on the following Monday. I finished out the week in a bleak mood and left the squadron on the Saturday morning. There was a small advantage that came with my new orders, I'd been given twenty-four hours leave between postings. In the hope of some excitement, I decided to spend it in London. To mark my departure from the squadron, an impromptu party was held in the Officers' Mess and we did our best to drink the bar dry. I'd made some friends at Manston, but my time there had largely been shrouded in miserable weather and arguments, I was glad to be moving on. With no idea what my next posting would bring me, I was in an anxious and slightly hazy mood when I climbed into my Bentley the following morning and started the engine.

I'd acquired the car on my last squadron, it had belonged to my flight commander who'd been killed in action. With its three and a half litre engine and long chassis it was a difficult machine to handle. In cold weather it wasn't very comfortable, the canvas hood was barely waterproof and the wind would attack you from all sides. However, it had a great turn of speed and I enjoyed the challenge of keeping all four wheels on the road. Privately, I also held a strong emotional connection between the car and a lost comrade.

Just as I pulled up to the Guardroom and waited for the sentry to raise the barrier, I noticed a figure running towards me in the mirror. It was a plump woman wearing a WAAF uniform. By the time she reached the car she was red faced and out of breath.

"Sir, sir!" she shouted. "This arrived for you." She handed me a large parcel wrapped in brown paper. I thanked her and placed it on the passenger seat.

It was just after eleven o'clock when I drove through the station gates. There was a cold nip in the air which did nothing to help my hangover. I took the main road towards Rochester. All being well, I estimated it would take a good two hours to get to London. Apart from the odd cart and van the road was quiet and I was able to keep up a constant speed. After an hour or so I stopped at a roadside café and was served a mug of tea by a large woman wearing an apron. After stretching my legs and consulting a map, I motored on and reached the outskirts of the city.

The country had been at war for eighteen months and the signs of conflict were all about. Sandbags, air-raid shelters and machine gun posts were commonplace. Like most of the population these fortifications had become very familiar to me, but I was quite unprepared for the devastated landscape that lay in front of me.

Just outside of Deptford was a barren plot of land where an enormous warehouse had been destroyed by the bombing. Further on was another bombsite and then a row of terrace houses sliced cleanly through the middle. Everywhere I looked there were ruined buildings. London had been hit hard over the last six months. Even after the Battle of Britain had been decided the Luftwaffe had pressed on relentlessly with their attacks. Several large scale raids in November and December decimated parts of the Capital. I'd seen the pictures in the newspapers and at the cinema, but those two-dimensional black and white images couldn't convey the true extent of the damage wrought upon the area.

I drove slowly through this eerie landscape. It was the tidiness that disturbed me most. Evidently these sites had been bombed a while ago, since then the roads had been cleared and the rubble and debris had been heaped up neatly. Usually, a building falls into dereliction over a period of time and vegetation slowly takes hold, but here, nature hadn't yet been able to claim back the ground. Everything was stark and dusty like the surface of an alien planet devoid of life.

Ahead on the horizon, sections of a ruined building stood up proudly like obelisks in the late morning mist. Again, more rows of gutted houses. A three floor tenement block had been smashed open exposing the interior like a broken doll's house. I wondered what had happened to the occupants. Were they safe or lying dead somewhere under all that rubble?

The air that filtered in through my hood smelt musty and clung to the back of my throat. As I drove on I noticed several gangs of workmen. There was no urgency about them, the danger of the raids had long since passed. A few shops were still open, others had been badly damaged and the proprietors were trading from barrows and carts in the open air.

At Bermondsey I saw where a large factory had burnt to the ground. Two of its walls still stood, the red bricks blackened by fire. In the centre charred timbers lay across each other like the contents of a giant ashtray.

I crossed over Tower Bridge and the Pool of London where merchant ships lay shoulder to shoulder in the busy docks. On the northern side of the Thames the old part of the city had also been ravaged. Just after Christmas a mass of incendiary bombs had been dropped here and a huge firestorm had ripped through the area. They called it the second great fire of London.

I was shocked to see the medieval church that stood at the top of Tower Hill had been badly damaged. Although I had no formal connection with the parish, the church was very familiar to me. My father had a small etching of it hanging in our hallway and as a child the print had always fascinated me. I almost wept when I saw the roof and interior had been burnt away.

I was too naive to properly comprehend the politics behind the war. I was young and emotional, and all this desolation angered me. How could we let this happen? I dropped a gear and accelerated away in a furious temper.

I passed under the shadow of St Paul's, up Ludgate Hill, through Fleet Street and into the Strand. In this area the evidence of war was still apparent, but the bomb damage was far less and the city was very much alive. I found a narrow side street and parked the Bentley. I picked up my kit bag and parcel and walked round the corner to the Strand Palace Hotel.

I had telegraphed ahead and booked a night at the hotel. This was a luxury far beyond my budget, but I'd become complacent in my spending habits. Too many of my comrades had been killed over the past year and I'd judged it was better to die with an empty bank account and pocket full of I.O.U.s than to leave anything behind. I had by, my reckoning, just enough money for a good night in town.

The entrance to the hotel was an extraordinary statement of Art Deco. Great panels of frosted glass were joined with neat beads of brass and steel. The reception desk was manned by an immaculately dressed man.

"Good morning sir," he had a strong French accent.

"Hello, I've booked a room." I swung my kit bag from my shoulder. The Frenchman's eyes assessed me with an air of continental distain.

"What name?"

"Sommers, Pilot Officer Sommers."

He consulted the large ledger on the desk.

"Ah yes. You are on the second floor, room two hundred and eight." From the mahogany pigeonholes behind him he took a key and handed it to me. He snapped his fingers sharply and from an alcove an elderly porter with white hair and pinched lips stepped forward.

"'Fraid the lift's not working," he rasped as he struggled to pick up my bag. I followed him towards the main staircase and up to the second floor. We reached my room and he opened the door for me. He laid my parcel on the bed and the kit bag on the floor.

"Bathroom's down there, second door on the left." He pointed down the hallway. "And breakfast is served from seven."

The room was small and sparsely furnished, but more than adequate for my needs. After the porter closed the door I opened the parcel. Folded neatly inside was a heavy overcoat or 'greatcoat'. On top was a small card with the tailor's name and underneath was a handwritten note. The script read – With the compliments of Mr and Mrs Sommers; it was a present from my parents.

I took out the coat and held it up. It was made of heavy blue-grey wool that matched my uniform. On the shoulders, two pilot officer stripes were set proudly on the epaulettes. Inside, the lining was cut from rayon that shimmered in the light. Set down the double-breasted front were eight brass buttons, each embossed with a crown and eagle. It was undoubtedly the finest article of clothing that I'd ever owned and must have cost my father a fair sum of money.

I unpacked, shaved and changed my shirt. I wrote a quick note to my parents to thank them for the coat and sent a telegram to a friend I was hoping to meet. It was still early, but I didn't want to sit around in the hotel lounge, so I headed out.

Outside Charing Cross Station I bought two packets of Dunhill cigarettes from a tobacconist and then ordered a pot of tea in a Corner House. Through the window I watched a policeman standing in the middle of the junction and conducting the flow of traffic like a well-seasoned maestro. I fidgeted with my watch and checked the time again. I'd become so accustomed to an operational lifestyle that I found it difficult to sit still and relax when on leave.

In Trafalgar square I was tempted by a concert at the National Gallery, but my restless mind was in need of something far more cheerful than Chopin in E Minor. Instead, I wandered up to the Empire Cinema and bought a ticket for Gone with the Wind. I'd seen the film before, but it was warm in the theatre and I was more than happy to stare at Viven Leigh in glorious Technicolor. About two hours later as the credits rolled and the music swelled, I woke up. I was surprised, I had no idea I'd fallen asleep.

I ambled back to the hotel in the gloom of early evening. A reply to my telegram was waiting for me at the reception desk. It read: GOOD TO SEE YOU'RE IN TOWN STOP MEET FOR DRINKS PUNCH TAVERN SIX PM STOP FANSHAW STOP.

I'd met James Fanshaw when I was stationed at North Weald. He was a journalist and one of the most colourful characters I'd ever known. He was good company and great entertainment, although there was always something suspicious about him. He was the kind of man you could trust with your life but not with your secrets.

I found the Punch Tavern amongst the newspaper offices at the end of Fleet Street. It was a classic old London pub with high ceilings, dark wood panelling and a musty smell of old tobacco smoke. Fanshaw stood amongst a group of men in the public bar and was engaged in an intense conversation, one of his hands was thumping the counter while the other held a gin and tonic. He had the appearance of a well dressed man at the end of a very hard day. Under his dark grey worsted suit his tie was loosened and his top button, as always, was undone. He spotted me coming in and shouted across the room.

"Hang on to your wallet and don't say a thing! This place is crawling with disreputable journalists." There were groans and cries from his fellow drinkers.

"Just like you!"

"That's true, I am a journalist." He straightened his back. "But I'm reputable." This prompted further laughs and cat calls from along the bar. He stepped aside from the group then greeted me with a firm handshake and slap on the back.

"So, what brings you to town?"

"I've got a short spell of leave and I'm making the most of it."

"Good, we've got a table at seven. What's your poison?" He turned to the barman.

"I'll have a G and T as well,"

"I'm very sorry sir, we're just out of gin," the barman replied with a regretful frown.

"Pity, I think I had the last drop," Fanshaw apologised. "Damn nuisance this war."

I reluctantly opted for a pint of best bitter instead. Fanshaw then introduced me to the group he was with, mostly journalists who wrote for the national newspapers. He went on to tell me that he was now working for a news agency and had been promised a big assignment. In the meantime, he was writing stories which were being syndicated in the States.

"Trouble is, everyone's writing the same old guff," he

explained. "It's always the same with big events, I want to be digging around for something different and exclusive. I'm getting bored with writing about tough old Londoners being bombed."

"I drove through the East End earlier. I was amazed at the damage there."

"It was bloody awful. One night they stuck me on a fire watch with a photographer. We ended up on a rooftop watching the sky turn red. I've never seen anything so terrifying as I did that night, it was as if the end of the world was upon us." He sipped his drink, then said dismissively, "But those stories are weeks old now. And most of them have been turned into propaganda pieces aimed at dragging the Americans in."

"Do you think they'll get involved?"

"Not directly, but the word is that Churchill has made a deal with them to supply weapons and equipment. You might find yourself buzzing around in a Yankee kite soon!"

His comment intrigued me and I conjured up an image of flying some exotic American aircraft.

"That's good news," I remarked enthusiastically.

"Depends on how you look at it. Yes, we need the equipment and we need them as an ally, but we're going to end up in debt to them for a long time." I admired Fanshaw's intelligence, he always managed to find a different angle which challenged the general view on current affairs.

"So, what have you been up to recently?" he asked casually.

"Not much. Patrolling back and forth across the south

coast mainly." I was always cautious when talking about operations in public, but with Fanshaw around I was even more guarded. He had a way of slipping subtle questions into a pleasant conversation and before you knew it you'd given more information away than you should have.

"Have you been over the Channel at all?"

"Oh no, I'm not falling for your game. Last time I told you something I found myself in a bloody magazine," I laughed. "Besides, I don't know if you're a German spy."

"Hey, that magazine article did you good. You know we had a string of girls contact the office asking for your address."

"Really? They never told me that," I said with surprise.

"That's because we couldn't pass on any information about you. You know careless talk costs lives and all that." Fanshaw rocked back on his heels and gave a wry smile.

"Well regardless, I'm not telling you anything. I'm here to enjoy an evening in the city." I'd taken off my greatcoat and I noticed he was looking at the purple and white medal ribbon above my breast pocket.

"Good to see you've got that sewn on."

"Don't remind me," I sighed. "It's given me no end of grief."

"Oh really, why's that?"

"I get a lot of stick about it." I glanced down at the ribbon. "I've come to the conclusion that medals are best worn discreetly."

"But you bloody well deserved it."

"Did I? I was just doing my job and happened to get lucky. Quite frankly I find the damn thing an embarrassment."

"Yes, there is something to be said for carrying out one's duty without honour or reward." Fanshaw gave me a curious look which I couldn't understand. "Still, it's an impressive piece to flash in front of a lady."

"I wouldn't know, I haven't had the chance to try it out yet."

"We can see how it works tonight then. I asked a couple of girls from the Admiralty to join us. One's an old friend of mine and she's bringing a pal along." He winked as he finished the sentence. Excitement flickered inside me as I considered the potential of female company. Manston had not been the most sociable posting and I was looking forward to having some fun.

"Where are we heading?" I asked.

"We've got a table at a nice French place off Shoe Lane. The proprietor is a funny little man, his wife does all the cooking. But a word of warning, make sure you keep away from his daughter."

"As long as the food is hot, I don't care."

"It will be. Here's a good bit of advice, most of the London restaurants are struggling with rationing so always look for French places. I tell you, what they produce from meagre ingredients is amazing. The trouble with us British is we had too much good food for too long and never really learnt how to cook, but the French, they could make the leg of a farmyard dog look appetising on a bed of sautéed potatoes."

We sunk a second round of drinks before heading over to the restaurant. It was dark by then and the city was smothered by the blackout. It was the second winter of air raid precautions where external lights were either switched off or restricted. Regardless of the darkness, the city was still teeming with people. The stoic Londoners seemed to have developed some form of sixth sense which allowed them to navigate the streets without light.

Tucked away on the corner of a narrow alley was the restaurant. It was a small place with square tables covered in red and white gingham cloths. The gas lamps were down low with candles on the tables providing most of the light.

It wasn't long before we were joined by the girls from the Admiralty. Fanshaw's date was an attractive slim blonde; her friend was a brunette with a pretty face and fuller figure. Both wore the black WREN's uniform with matching stockings, they were charming and sophisticated.

The evening started well. As Fanshaw predicted the French cuisine was delicious, but the proprietor was rude and irritable. We split the bill between the two of us. I could hardly afford to do so, but I felt my prospects were good and considered this an investment that might pay dividends later in the evening. Afterwards Fanshaw suggested we moved onto a nightclub. His knowledge of London night life was second to none. He knew where to find the best food, the best music, the best drinks and always the best atmosphere. I suggested he should publish a guidebook.

"You'd make a fortune."

"But that, dear chap, would be giving all my secrets away." He shook his head.

However, despite my efforts and investment my ambitions for the evening were thwarted by a cavalry officer who not only out ranked me but also had considerably better financial resources.

In the early hours of Sunday morning Fanshaw and I tumbled out of the nightclub into the freezing smog.

"Where did the girls go?" he asked me in a drunken slur.

"I lost mine about an hour ago, where's yours?"

"She's gone! A big city banker whisked her away in a Rolls Royce."

We said our goodbyes and somehow I made it back to the safety of my hotel room. I was late waking the next morning and in no fit state to eat breakfast. I lay under the covers, drifting in and out of sleep until my stomach settled and I was able to stand up straight. I'd slept completely naked, my uniform was crumpled in a heap at the foot of the bed.

As I started to dress, I realised to my horror that I had mislaid my greatcoat. In a blind fury I ransacked the room in the hope that it was hidden somewhere under the mess, but it wasn't there. I sat on the edge of the bed and tried to recall what had happened. My memory of the night before was so hazy I couldn't remember if I was wearing it when I arrived back at the hotel.

Downstairs, I asked a young girl on reception to check if it had been handed in, but all they had in lost property was an old umbrella. I retraced my steps back to the Punch Tavern, where the landlord shook his head and said he hadn't seen it. In the restaurant I had to use my schoolboy French to try and explain what I was looking for, but they couldn't help either. With some difficulty I managed to find the nightclub, but it was shut and locked and after banging on the door for nearly twenty minutes there was no answer.

I was furious with myself and deeply upset. I penned a note to Fanshaw asking if he could make enquiries on my behalf and left it at his office. In the middle of the afternoon I had to give up and accept that because of my own stupidity my greatcoat was gone for good. It had been an expensive night out. Feeling utterly dejected I climbed into the Bentley, started the engine and headed out of the city.

# Chapter 4

## Number 2 Camouflage Unit

As I left London and my greatcoat behind, I started to consider my immediate future. I had no idea what I'd be doing at Heston. My greatest fear was being moved on to a training unit as an instructor. I could think of nothing more tedious and frustrating. Even though the Rhubarb operations had been badly organised they did put me on the front line and in the thick of action.

Heston was an hour's drive along the Great West Road. I took it at a leisurely cruise as fuel was getting low and my financial reserves were somewhat depleted.

The weather had brightened up, but it was still bitterly cold and no matter how I tried to cover up, the wind whipped around inside the hood and nipped at the nape of my neck. After a few wrong turns I found the airfield. I'd expected to see the standard metal gates and brick guardhouse that formed the entrance to most RAF stations, but Heston was very different. A wide sweeping road led up to a makeshift barrier. A telegraph pole wrapped in barbed wire, barred the way. To the side stood a corrugated iron shelter. As I approached a soldier appeared from within. He ambled over with a lazy stride and a grim expression on his face.

"Afternoon sir," he pushed his head under the canvas hood and peered into the back of the car to check I was alone.

"I'm reporting in," I replied brusquely.

"Can I see your identification please?" This time I had my papers, I drew them out from my uniform tunic and handed them over. He thumbed through the documents with his fingerless gloves and then gave a grunt which I took to mean he was happy with my credentials. He gave me back the papers and with a shrill whistle signalled to another soldier to push the barrier open.

"Where's the station HQ?" I asked. He shrugged his shoulders nonchalantly.

"I'd try up there," he pointed towards a complex of buildings at the end of the road. "That's where the officer's accommodation is." I jerked the car into gear and pulled away.

As the aerodrome was quiet I took the opportunity to drive around the buildings and see if there was any clue as to what I would be doing there.

The most prominent structure was the control tower which sat on top of a rectangular building with two long wings. According to the sign outside this was the club house and hotel. On either side was a series of sizable hangars and a large area of grass which made up the main airfield and runways. I was impressed at the size and quality of the infrastructure, I'd become used to slumming it in drafty wooden sheds. Looking about I expected to see some form of activity, but apart from a man mending a bicycle outside one of the hangars there was no one about. I turned left and followed a concrete road which ran behind the buildings. I was pleased to see the firm roadway, a blessed relief after the mud of Manston.

At the eastern end of the road was a hangar that was larger than the others and out of keeping with the rest of the architecture. As I turned the Bentley around I noticed the side entrance was guarded by a sentry. He eyed me curiously as I read the sign above his head, Number 2 Camouflage Unit. So, this was the unit I was to report to on the following day. It all seemed very suspicious. Why would it be guarded?

I motored back up to the hotel and parked up amongst an eclectic mix of vehicles. Two Humber staff cars in drab green sat side by side,. Next to them was a small Morris van painted matt black, a BSA motorcycle and then a large Rolls Royce Phantom with burgundy coachwork. I wondered if it belonged to the banker who'd stolen Fanshaw's date. Inside I was greeted at the reception desk by a young man in a civilian suit.

"Checking in sir?" he asked.

"Yes I think so, I've got orders to report here." The young man took a pencil and gently ran it down a piece of paper on the desk.

"Yes, here you are. Pilot Officer Sommers." I was taken aback, how did he know my name? Then I realised it was stencilled in large letters on the kit bag I was holding over my shoulder. He took a key from a brass hook and gave it to me.

"We've given you room eight. Second floor, last door on the left." He pointed a delicate finger towards the room alongside. "The bar opens at six. Breakfast and dinner are both served in the restaurant."

The club house was the finest accommodation I'd ever been posted to. It was well appointed with modern décor and a plush carpet on the second floor. Along the corridor framed photographs of different aircraft hung under frosted glass downlighters. My mood brightened, for whatever lay in store for me at least I would be comfortable.

My room was spacious with two beds, a wardrobe and an armchair. A large metal framed window looked north over the airfield. I threw my kit bag down, unbuttoned my tunic and kicked off my shoes. I laid down on one of the beds and studied my feet. A hole had appeared on the end of my right sock and my big toe was poking through. I stretched out and put my hands behind my head.

A little while later I was aroused from a shallow sleep by the door opening. A thin wiry man holding a kit bag like mine entered nervously.

"Hi, hello," he spoke with a neat, clipped accent. "I'm very sorry they told me I'm to share this room with you."

"Well, it looks like we're bunk mates then." I sprung up from the bed and introduced myself. "I'm Jack Sommers."

"I'm Richards, Geoffrey Richards." We shook hands. I estimated he was slightly older than me, his dark hair was swept back and already starting to recede. Like myself he was a pilot officer, but he wore no medals under his pilot's brevet.

"I've been told to report to the Camouflage Unit," he

explained.

"I've got the same orders, looks like we're on the same job. Any idea what they do here?" He gave a shrug of the shoulders.

"I'm afraid not, this is my first operational posting."

"Where have you come from?" I enquired.

"Sutton Bridge, OTU." This was worrying, if he had come directly from an operational training unit, he had no combat experience.

After we'd both unpacked and settled in, we headed down to the bar. It was a large room built for entertaining, but apart from an army officer who sat reading a broadsheet, the place was empty. A woman was cleaning glasses behind the bar.

"Won't be a moment," she dried the last glass and reached up to place it on a rack. "Right, what will it be?"

We ordered two pints of best bitter and I offered Richards one of my Dunhills.

"Is your room okay?" the woman asked as she pulled on the pump and the beer gurgled into the dimpled glass.

"Yes, very nice thank you," answered Richards.

"Is it always this quiet?" I asked her.

"It's mainly civilians here, a lot of them live off site, so the weekends are always quiet." She placed a pint in front of Richards. "If you need anything while you're here just ask me or Charlie on the desk. I'm Pimm by the way." She was an attractive brunette, in early middle age. A dark blue cotton dress hugged her figure and the diamond on her wedding ring glinted as it caught the light. She smiled and went back to cleaning the glasses.

Halfway through our drinks another pilot entered the bar. He was well built with a square jawline and hair neatly combed to the side. With a purposeful stride he approached the bar and ordered a drink.

"Are you chaps stationed here?" he asked us.

"Just arrived," said Richards.

"Same here. I'm Chilton by the way." I offered him a drink. "So, are you on this strange camouflage business as well?" he asked lowering his voice. Richards gave a silent nod of the head.

"Any idea what we'll be doing?" We both shrugged our shoulders. Chilton went on, "I reckon it's night fighters, I've got a friend in the Ministry and he says they're forming a couple of new squadrons." It was an interesting suggestion, but I didn't agree with him and when I pressed him on the source of his information he became very vague.

We drank on and I quizzed Richards and Chilton about their flying experience. I was keen to know the calibre of the pilots I might be flying with and possibly going into combat alongside.

Both of them had joined up about six months after I had. Richards had been a trainee solicitor in a London law firm and Chilton was in his first year of University at Durham. Like Richards, this was Chilton's first operational posting. I hoped there would be some more experienced pilots on the unit as these two made me nervous, Chilton seemed a little too confident for his own good and something about Richards' awkward body language suggested he wasn't a natural fighter pilot. They were keen to hear about my own experiences, but I skirted their questions. I was always uncomfortable discussing my own achievements.

The following morning the atmosphere in the hotel had changed completely. The dining room was filled with people breakfasting. There were a few blue RAF uniforms, but most of the room was taken up with civilians. The three of us took a table by the window.

"I suppose that's where we were promised peace for our time." Richards was looking out across the tarmac apron that led onto the airfield. It suddenly dawned on me that this was where two years before, Neville Chamberlain, the then Prime Minister, had given his famous speech after returning from a meeting with Adolf Hitler. I'd remembered the newsreels showing him climbing out of an aircraft and waving a signed copy of the Munich agreement for all to see. The agreement provided for the German annexation of the Sudetenland where many ethnic Germans lived. At the time it was seen as a great triumph which extinguished the threat of war, but within months it had failed.

"That didn't work out, did it?" snorted Chilton as he buttered his toast. "Makes me laugh that Chamberlain thought he could stop the Germans with a piece of paper."

"I think war was coming anyway. All it did was prolong the inevitable." Richards commented. I kept quiet, politics was not a good subject for pilots to discuss. We needed to carry out orders and do the job without debating the policy.

As I reached for a small pot of marmalade I noticed a military policeman enter the dining room. He was a sergeant wearing khaki battledress and neat white webbing. On his arm was a red band with the letters MP printed in black. He spoke with the waiter who pointed towards us and to my astonishment he walked up to our table.

"Sorry to interrupt your breakfast sir," he said towering above me and then checking a scrap of paper in his hand. "I'm looking for a Pilot Officer Sommers." A succession of thoughts galloped through my brain. What had I done? Did I pay my bar bill last night? Was the Bentley parked in the wrong place? Had he found my greatcoat?

"Yes, …. that's me," I said cautiously.

"I'm also looking for Pilot Officers Richards and Chilton." The others looked nervously at him. "I've orders to escort you over to the hangars - when you've finished your breakfast, of course." A wave of relief spread over the table.

"I thought we were for the high jump then," whispered Chilton. We finished up as quickly as we could and headed outside where one of the Humber staff cars was waiting for us. We climbed in and the Sergeant started the engine.

"So, any idea what this is all about?" Chilton enquired.

"I couldn't say, sir." He pulled away and we sat in silence for the short journey across the airfield. The weather still looked bleak, with a stubborn layer of low cloud which was refusing to move. We stopped outside the large hangar I'd spotted the day before. This time the sentry came to attention and saluted as the three of us clambered out of the car. The Sergeant led us up to the entrance. By now I was very anxious to see what lay beyond the door and exactly what 'Number 2 Camouflage Unit' was all about.

We were shown into an office where a clerk with curly

hair and thick glasses asked us to sign our names in a ledger. He then opened another door and we filed into a briefing room.

"Please wait in here," he said, slamming the door shut.

The room was laid out with two tables pushed together in the centre and a set of folding wooden chairs tucked underneath. The floor was covered in dark lino tiles and the brick walls were painted in a two-tone scheme of dark green and cream. A Bell and Howell slide projector sat on the table and pointed towards a white canvas screen that was attached to the far wall. A well-used blackboard stood at the opposite end, stubs of chalk balanced on the top edge.

Through the windows, dismal sunlight struggled to illuminate the room. With a hard click Richards switched on the two lights that hung above the table. The feeble electric bulbs flickered in the fittings and did little to lift the miserable atmosphere. I spotted an ashtray on the windowsill and decided to light up. I offered a cigarette to Chilton.

"Not for me thanks." He stretched his arms out and then beat his chest. "I like to keep my lungs clear." We each pulled out a chair and sat down.

"What happens now?" asked Richards a rhetorical question if ever there was one. Chilton began to rhythmically tap the table with his forefinger. I looked around the room, there was no obvious clue as to what we were expected to do. Apart from the irritating sound of Chilton's drumming a full minute passed by in silence.

"I wonder what's through there?" I pointed to another door which I presumed opened into the main hangar.

"Bugger this," I hissed. I stubbed out my cigarette and was just about to get up and go exploring when the door flew open and two men walked in.

"Good morning gentlemen," said the first. He was wearing a grey mackintosh over his uniform, and the rank of Squadron Leader on his shoulders. He was middle aged with a rugged face, light grey hair and a moustache.

The second man was a Flight Lieutenant, slimmer with a bald head. Under his left arm he carried a large canvas map case which he placed on the table.

"Sorry about all this cloak and dagger business," said the Squadron Leader taking off his mackintosh to reveal a pilot's brevet and row of medals. "Trouble is, this is still a civilian airfield and we can't be too careful. That's why we've got our own security detachment." He nodded towards the door and then looked back at the table. "Did they not offer you any coffee?" Before any of us could answer he shouted for the clerk.

"Palmer!" The clerk opened the door and snapped to attention.

"Yes sir?"

"Can you get some coffee sorted, and it's bloody freezing in here, get that heating going will you?"

The clerk bent down below the window and started to fiddle with the valves on the gas fire. There was a hiss and then a pop as the flame took hold.

"All done sir." The clerk rose to his feet. "If it starts clanking give it a kick, that usually sorts it."

"Very good," the Squadron Leader muttered. He slumped himself down and waited for the clerk to leave the room and then looked up towards us.

"My name is Singleton and you'll be under my command for the foreseeable future. This is Flight Lieutenant Fenton, my second in command." He reached into the map case and pulled out a sheet of paper. He ran his eyes over some handwritten text and then looked at each of us. There was an alertness in his face and confidence in his voice.

"No doubt you're wondering what the hell's going on. I can now tell you that you've each been selected for special duties as photographic reconnaissance pilots."

With that, the cloud of mystery lifted. I was certainly surprised … although I wasn't sure if this was a good direction for my flying career to be taking. I looked across at Richards and Chilton. Both looked thoroughly confused.

"So, it's nothing to do with camouflage then?" asked Chilton.

"No, that's just a cover name for the unit here," Fenton explained with a shake of his head.

"Now, I assume you all know what photo reconnaissance means?" asked Singleton, each of us nodded back. "There's nothing new about the principle, we've been doing it for years, but what you won't know is how advanced the technology is and the methods we're now employing." He paused. "Don't underestimate the value of the operations you'll be tasked to carry out and don't underestimate the dangers involved. You'll be trained here for the next three weeks or until I think you are ready to be operational. Then you'll be posted to a PR unit and that could be anywhere we're fighting a war."

Photographic Reconnaissance was one of the first

military uses of aircraft. It was developed during the First World War as a simple idea - fly over the enemy trenches and photograph their movements. The trouble was the enemy was never really happy with this arrangement and often went to great lengths to shoot the aircraft down.

There was a knock at the door. The clerk entered with a tray of enamel mugs and flask of coffee. While we passed the flask around the table, Singleton took out a briar pipe and filled it from a tobacco pouch. He struck a match and lit the bowl. Sweet smelling smoke curled up towards the ceiling. There was something familiar about him, I had a feeling I'd seen him somewhere before.

Fenton moved the conversation on to practical issues, checking we'd all found our accommodation and explaining our daily routine. We would be training throughout the week, Saturday afternoons and Sundays would be our own. After nearly a year of erratic duty schedules this would be quite a change for me.

He told us that there was also an active PR unit and a roster of pilots stationed at Heston. Alongside the briefing room was a crew room and photographic interpretation facility, the latter was strictly off limits without permission. It was made clear to us that under no circumstances were we to get in the way of any operations either in the air or on the ground.

From the canvas map case Fenton produced three black and white photographic enlargements. Each was about ten by twelve inches in size with a black border and handwritten annotations scrawled across the bottom. The three images were aerial views of the same subject. From the mass of train lines which ran top to bottom it was easy to see it was a railway marshalling yard.

"This is a good example of the work you'll be doing." Fenton spoke with a hoarseness to his voice. "This is the railway yard at Laon in the Northeast of France. Each of these photographs was taken from an altitude of twenty-two thousand feet over a six day period." He pushed one of the photographs towards us. "Now, look at the first photograph, what can you see?"

"Lots of train lines …." Chilton murmured.

"Yes that's obvious," Fenton snapped, "but what's happening on those lines?" Like three diligent schoolboys we studied the image carefully. I could make out a series of rail sidings and long lines of flatbed wagons.

"The wagons look stationary to me, are they waiting for something?" I suggested.

"Yes they are, now look at the next photograph taken three days later." Fenton slid the second image over the first. The wagons were still in place, but now a line of vehicles had arrived.

"Are those tanks?" asked Richards tentatively.

"Yes, Panzer III Tanks to be precise," said Fenton. "We can tell that from their shape. In addition to that, because we know the altitude that the aircraft was flying at and the lens that was used, we can calculate the scale and then measure the vehicles." He dragged his finger over the glossy print. "If you count the number of tanks, you'll see there are sixty being loaded and there's another sixty lined up ready to go. That's an armoured brigade." He tapped the table. "Also, you can see the locomotive arrangement suggests the trains will head east." He moved on to the third image "This was taken forty-eight hours ago."

"They've all gone." Chilton exclaimed with a little surprise.

"Yes, so what we can deduce from the three pictures is that Jerry has moved a Panzer brigade out to the east. That could be a crucial piece of intelligence. If we had a secret agent on the ground it could take him days, maybe weeks, to get that information safely back to London. However, we can have it on a desk in Whitehall within a matter of hours."

I looked back at the second image and thought about the people on the ground, I wondered if they knew they were being photographed. Singleton took the pipe from his mouth and spoke.

"But the use of these images doesn't stop there. Say someone considered this to be a nice plump target for a bombing raid?" He pointed his thick finger at a round object in the bottom corner. "Look at these circles here, can you see what those are?"

I strained my eyes. The shape was familiar and instantly conjured up an image of the muzzle flashes that had blasted Gilroy out of the air on my last operation.

"Is that a flak battery? Twenty-millimetre?"

"Yes, I take it you've seen them before?" Singleton gave me a knowing look. "How the target is defended would be very useful information for a bomber crew. And of course, if we popped back after they've carried out the raid we could see how effective their efforts had been. So, you can see that the photographs you bring back will be of immense importance. You will be our spies in the skies."

Richards twisted awkwardly in his chair.

"When you say spies ...... if we're shot down would we be treated as spies?" he asked with concern.

"No," Fenton shook his head. "You'll be flying an aircraft with British markings and wearing uniform. If you are shot down you would be treated as a prisoner of war"

"As long as the enemy abides by the Geneva Convention." Singleton added.

"What aircraft would we be flying?" asked Chilton.

"That's the interesting bit." Singleton banged his pipe out on the ashtray and stood up. "Come through and have a look at this." We finished our coffee and he led us through the door into the hangar. Like all hangars it was a spacious building constructed from a series of steel girders that formed a clear span.  It was cluttered with different types of aircraft. Wingtips, propellers and rudder fins stuck out here and there. I was very curious to see what we would be flying, but my heart sank when I saw the nearest aircraft was an Airspeed Oxford, a twin-engine monoplane mainly used for training. It had its charm, but certainly wasn't the kind of machine I'd like to take into enemy territory.

"We use the Oxford for navigation training and testing equipment," said Singleton as he ducked under the wing. I sighed with relief and followed him. "This is what you'll be flying on operations." He pointed to a Spitfire that was tucked into the corner of the hangar. "You'll notice it's been specially modified." He was right, it was like the aircraft I'd been flying at Manston, but instead of the brown and green camouflage this one was painted in a pale shade of blue.

"Not too sure about the colour!" Chilton joked as we walked over towards it.

"The boffins at Farnborough have experimented with various different schemes and settled on blue as it's the best colour for high altitude work, it helps you blend in," explained Singleton. "Mind you, they said pink would be better against early morning skies." His moustache twitched with the hint of a smile. "She's powered by the new Rolls Royce Merlin 45." He tapped the engine cowling, then crouched down and pointed under the fuselage. "There are three cameras fitted to her. Two point directly down, that gives you a plan view when flying straight and level. The other is fixed behind the cockpit and points out horizontally. That's called the oblique and gives you a much better image at low level." He used his hands to demonstrate the different angles of view. "There are also a few differences around the cockpit. The canopy has special blisters which give better visibility and obviously inside you've got the camera controls." My eye ran along the leading edge of the wing and I noticed there were no gun ports.

"What armament is she equipped with?" I inquired.

"None," replied Singleton.

"But how do we defend ourselves?" asked Chilton sharply.

"Run like hell!" Singleton smiled. "With these PR Spitfires all eight machine guns, the firing mechanisms, the ammunition and the armoured plating have been removed. That reduces their weight by about five hundred pounds. Which means they are very fast, in fact one of the fastest aircraft types in the world. So, if you're unlucky enough to find a Messerschmitt on your tail, push the throttle forward and you'll be gone before they can get a bead on you." He leant against the wing and looked back at us. "Your best means of survival will be speed and navigation. Get in, snap away with the camera and get out quick."

"Does the weight affect the range?" asked Richards.

"Yes that's the other advantage of taking the weapons out. We can increase the fuel load. With the tanks filled you'll be able to cover nearly two thousand miles. That's more than enough for a trip to Berlin and back."

"Bloody hell," exclaimed Chilton. I shared his sentiment. The idea of being that deep into occupied Europe alone and unarmed was distinctly alarming.

"There's a few other quirks about the aircraft," explained Singleton. "With the weight removed you'll find the centre of gravity different from the other Spitfires you've flown and they're very sensitive on the throttle."

We spent some time examining the airframe in detail and then headed back into the briefing room where Fenton ran through our training programme.

"With regard to your time here at Heston, there are three key elements. The first is understanding the principles of aerial photography, the second is navigation and finally you'll need to show that you're familiar with both the aircraft and equipment."

He went on to explain that we would start with sorties in the Airspeed Oxford. Its fuselage had been converted to hold the same type of camera system installed in the Spitfires. After that, we would spend time learning how to plan our operations and fly a series of exercises over training targets. Just before we broke for lunch, Fenton issued a stern warning.

"This will be an intense programme. We need capable pilots. If you don't come up to scratch, I'll send you straight back to your units."

# Chapter 5

## Back to school

The rest of the morning rushed by in a blur of formalities. Our logbooks were scrutinised, medical records checked and various papers were signed. After a hurried lunch break, Fenton sent us to the back of the hangar where the maintenance crew had set out a line of workbenches. Two erks were busy inspecting an electric motor and another was beating a bent aluminium panel back into shape. Watching over them was Flight Sergeant Morgan, a portly man with a bright red face. As the senior non-commissioned officer, he was responsible for all the maintenance of the aircraft and equipment. He greeted us with an oil stained clipboard in his hands and a scowl across his face.

"So, you lot want to fly my aeroplanes," he pronounced the 'a' as an 'h'. "Come over here," he wheezed, with little regard for our rank. We dutifully followed him to one of the benches where a large metal box stood. It was about two and half feet long, with one end being square and the other circular.

"I've been told to show you the equipment you'll be

using. But before I do, I think it's best you know that I don't like aircrew touching or interfering with anything they shouldn't." He put down the clipboard and picked up the box.

"This then is the F-24 camera. You'll find three of them mounted on each Spitfire." He turned the camera upright. "Just like your box brownie that you take your holiday snaps on it's got a lens here." He pointed to the circular end. "Which projects the light onto a film plane here." His podgy finger ran up the device. "It uses different lenses for taking pictures at different heights. So, when you plan your operation you need to tell your ground crew what height you'll be wanting to take the pictures at and they will attach the correct lens." With a snap he unclipped the top cover. "It takes a roll of five inch wide film which goes in here and can take two hundred and fifty exposures on one can. The camera is controlled in the cockpit by a switch that powers an electric motor." He slammed the cover shut.

"Don't touch or adjust anything on the camera yourself. Leave it to your ground crew. There is only one circumstance when you should need to touch the camera. That is if you're unlucky enough to crash land in enemy territory. As you know, if you and the aircraft are still in one piece the standard procedure is to set fire to the airframe. However, if you can't do that for whatever reason, get into the camera compartment, remove the film magazine and expose the film to the light. That will bugger up any photos you've taken." He demonstrated the method by removing the magazine and showing us the mechanism.

"When you return after an operation one of the erks will

be on hand to immediately remove the camera. I repeat, don't touch it yourself." In my experience I'd found that ground crew were often overly possessive of their aircraft and equipment, Morgan was no exception. He went on to show us the intricate heating system that prevented the cameras from icing up at high altitude and the extra fuel tanks that had been installed. Before he finished he puffed out his chest and gave us a warning.

"Be careful when you come back from an operation, you might find a lot of the intelligence men waiting for you. Some of them have a tendency to get very excited and can get in the way. They might be intelligent, but that doesn't mean they have any common sense. Try not to run them over. The last thing I want is blood and guts all over my aeroplanes."

"The weather looks like it might be better tomorrow," said Singleton back in the briefing room. "So, we'll get up in the Oxford and you can see how the cameras work. Report here after breakfast with your flying gear. Don't forget your passes or they won't let you in." As we got up to leave Singleton called me back. "Sommers I'll run you back in my car," I stood aside and let the others file through the door.

Outside it was dark, but the clouds had thinned and a handful of stars were dotted about the sky. Singleton climbed into his Rover and reached across to unlock the passenger door for me.

"I had a good look at your operational record. It's very impressive." He started the engine and twisted the switch on the dashboard to bring on the headlamps. "I hope you're not disappointed about being posted here."

"I must admit it was a bit of a shock, sir." I didn't see any harm in being honest.

"The thing is we need men with experience." He pulled away and the headlights swung out across the dark airfield. "It's likely that this job is going to open up some very interesting opportunities and once you've finished here you'll be in great demand. So, don't get disheartened." He turned and grinned at me. "I want you to assume the role of senior pilot and help these other chaps along. Strictly confidentially, both of them were falling short of the mark and they wouldn't have made it onto a fighter squadron. But I think they've got potential."

"I was relieved to see we've got Spitfires. I was worried you'd send us plodding over the Channel in some old biplane."

"Yes, the technology has improved immensely. You know, only a year ago I was flying Fairey Battles in France. In those old buses the observer had to hang out of the back cockpit and hold the bloody camera in his hands. We didn't have the speed or the range."

I'd heard horrific stories of the Fairey Battles. They were slow, cumbersome aircraft that had been easy prey for the German fighters. In a mere four days fighting over France sixty Fairey Battles were destroyed: just over half of the attacking force. Singleton had obviously been in the thick of the slaughter and was lucky to have survived. We reached the clubhouse and he pulled over.

"I live off the station so I'll drop you here."

"Good night, sir." I said slamming the door shut.

The bar was busy that evening. I found Richards and

Chilton by the fireplace. Richards was sitting forward with his elbows on his knees and a cigarette between his fingers. Chilton had pushed himself back in an armchair with his legs sprawled out across the floor.

"How's about that," said Richards as I pulled up a chair. "My head's swimming after what we've been told today."

"That was a lot to take in," I agreed.

"Oh, I don't know," Chilton remarked flippantly. "I think it's all pretty straightforward stuff."

Pimm appeared with a tray of drinks that I had ordered from the bar.

"Here we go lads," she said with a smile. I stood up and took the drinks from her. As she turned away I caught the sweet aroma of her perfume.

"That new Spitfire looks like a bit of a handful." Richards seemed genuinely overwhelmed by what we'd been shown.

"Nonsense, the more power you've got, the better the aircraft." Chilton waved his hands dismissively. "If you get into trouble, bang the throttle forward and power out." I glowered at him, his cocksure attitude was starting to aggravate me again.

After another round of drinks I headed upstairs for an early night. On my way through, Charlie, the young man on reception, stopped me.

'Sir, a letter arrived for you.' He handed me an envelope with 'On His Majesty's Service' printed in blue ink across the top. Charlie was staring at me inquisitively, I stared back at him and he looked away. I tore the envelope open expecting to find some further orders about my posting, but instead it was a typed memo from the equipment store at RAF North Weald. The curtly worded text informed me that I needed to return the flying boots I'd signed for last year or I would be charged accordingly. I smirked, I had no idea what had happened to those boots. Both of them had been lost when I'd bailed out of a Hurricane. I studied the envelope. How on earth did a stores clerk know I was here?

As I lay in bed I wondered what the future held. Was this a bad posting for me? I couldn't tell. Had I stayed on a frontline squadron, I might have been promoted to flight commander, then maybe a Squadron Leader, but that was a very ambitious thought.

There had been a lot of concern about pilots becoming fatigued and then burning out. I knew some of the men I'd flown with last year had been moved into training units and at least one had been taken off operations completely. I didn't think any of them would win medals teaching students circuits and bumps. At least being a photo reconnaissance pilot meant I'd still be operational. On reflection I decided it was best to hunker down and give this posting my best shot. Besides, there was a danger that if I rested on my laurels I could find myself in a worse situation.

Beyond my career prospects there were two other elements in this opportunity that interested me. The first was Singleton. He was an aviator from the old school, the kind of man I found easy to follow and find an affinity with. The second was that pale blue Spitfire, the fastest machine on earth.

The beating throb of a Merlin engine woke me early the

next morning. I rolled out of bed and pulled back the curtain just in time to see the thin silhouette of a Spitfire climbing into the sunrise. I looked down across the grass, it was cold outside and patches of frost were glistening as the early morning sun touched the ground.

After breakfast we all gathered in the briefing room where Fenton had laid out a mass of charts and maps across the table.

"Your exercise today is going to involve planning and navigating an operation over Bristol." He walked over to the blackboard and picked up a stub of chalk. "When planning a PR sortie it's important to remember the moment you get near to the enemy coastline you could be watched, and we don't want Jerry to know what you're photographing. So, you plan your routes to avoid giving the game away." He drew a squiggly line which I took to represent the coast of Northern Europe. "Say that you're tasked with photographing a target here." With two firm strokes he drew a cross in the middle of the continent. "What you don't do is to fly straight to the target, turn around and come back. That would make the target pretty obvious. Instead, you plan a route which takes you over several different targets. He chalked out another two crosses and then joined them up with a crooked line. "This way they won't know which target you're really interested in. The chances are you'll be sent out to photograph the same target on different days. In which case you alter the course drastically for each day. Say that on the first day you might come in high over France, pass over the target and then turn north to run out over the Netherlands. The second day you might come in over Belgium and then fly out the way you came in."

"What about flak? How do we know where to avoid?" I asked, thinking about Gilroy again.

"Unless the batteries have been forewarned you should be okay. The twenty mill won't bother you at high altitude and you should be too small and fast for the eighty-eights. Besides, a few quick turns should throw them off." I didn't find the complacency in his answer reassuring.

We all set to work and planned a route for our exercise which would take us northwest for seventy miles then southwest across the Cotswolds before turning due south towards Bristol. We would fly the course at eight thousand feet, but ten miles out from the target we would drop to five thousand feet and make a flat pass directly over the town. I jotted down the figures and calculated it to be a round trip of one hundred and fifty-five miles and estimated a flying time of fifty-eight minutes.

"Should be easy," scoffed Chilton.

"Yes, it should be. So, there's no reason to screw it up," sighed Fenton. It was amusing to see that Chilton's attitude was getting on his nerves as well as mine.

In the crew room we put on our flying gear. I liked to be unrestricted when flying so I'd taken to removing my tie, undoing my top shirt button and wearing a thick woollen jumper under my leather jacket. Apart from keeping me warm in a cold cockpit, where there were always numerous draughts, it gave a more casual appearance, which appealed to my rebellious side. Richards wore his bulky leather jacket over the top of his uniform. I watched him as we walked outside, he looked ungainly and his movements were almost arthritic.

The erks had pulled the Oxford out of the hangar. Singleton was waiting for us, wearing a grubby white flying suit and leaning against the wing.

"Sommers you'll be upfront with me." He opened the little triangular door on the fuselage and climbed in. I followed, being careful not to put my foot through the delicate fabric covering. It was a tight squeeze in the fuselage and I had to stoop low. The centre of the aircraft was taken up with a mass of equipment. Wires and cables spilled out of three metal boxes. I recognised one of the F-24 cameras we had been told not to touch by Flight Sergeant Morgan. I squeezed through towards the cockpit. Being the pilot in command Singleton had taken the left hand seat. I waited for him to adjust his straps before I climbed into the seat beside him.

"Right, I'll get her airborne, beyond that you'll have control."

I was to fly and navigate the course and then instruct Richards and Chilton in the back when we were approaching the target. They would operate the camera equipment under the watch of Fenton. I'd then continue back to Heston and if the weather held, we would change positions and repeat the process.

"You ever flown a twin engine aircraft before?" asked Singleton.

"No, afraid not sir."

"Okay, she's fairly straight forward. You probably find her a bit docile and heavy, so keep her well trimmed."

As we waited for the others to settle in I noticed a Spitfire coming into land, I assumed it was the one I'd seen take off earlier. It touched down gently and then taxied up to the hangar in front of us.

"That's Rowbotham back from a jaunt. He's one of the most experienced pilots we've got," said Singleton as he began to run through the pre-flight checks. The pilot of the Spitfire shut the engine down, and two erks ran up to the fuselage. I watched them open the camera bay door and carefully remove the film cannisters. Before the pilot had been able to unstrap himself the cannisters were already on their way to the darkroom for developing. Over in the corner I noticed a dispatch rider resting on the seat of his motorcycle. He was obviously waiting to run the developed photographs to wherever they were needed.

Singleton started the Oxford's engines and we moved off the chocks. He was a natural pilot, it was a pleasure to watch him gently coax the aircraft down the runway and into the air. At a thousand feet he gave me control of the aircraft.

He was right about the handling, there was a momentary lag between any input to the controls and the aircraft actually moving. The slow response was quite different from the fighters I'd been flying, but I quickly got used to it. Another difference I had to get my head around was monitoring two engines and keeping the throttles balanced, I'd only ever had one to worry about before. Apart from this I found the Oxford pleasant to fly. The cockpit had a great field of view and the seat was comfortable which made a big difference on a long trip.

I followed the course we had planned and came in straight and level over Cirencester. Being blessed with fair weather and good visibility, it was hardly a test of my navigational skills. In the afternoon we rotated around and flew the course again, this time with Chilton in the co-pilot's seat. I sat in the back with the camera equipment between my legs. There was a small hole in the floor of the fuselage, through this I could gauge the position of the aircraft and when to start taking photographs. Over the intercom Chilton kept me informed of our position.

"Okay, we're coming up on the target." Looking down I could see fields and woods passing underneath, then two houses, and then a few more. I readied myself.

"Now," he shouted over the intercom. I pressed the switch on the camera controls and the motor whirred away.

It was difficult to judge Chilton's flying abilities as I was facing rearwards, but apart from a few course corrections he seemed to do well. It was pretty dull work in the back of the aircraft and after a while I began to feel nauseous, it was a relief to get back to Heston.

By the time we rotated around for the last sortie the sky had become very overcast. Over Bicester the visibility was dramatically decreased. Richards was now in the co-pilot's seat and he was struggling to keep on course. A couple of times I felt the aircraft turn erratically and assumed he was trying to get back on the correct bearing. Over the intercom I could hear the conversation between the pilots.

"If you're worried about your position what do you need to do?" Singleton asked as if he was a teacher ushering a pupil through an exam.

"I'm looking for a landmark." There was a hint of panic in Richards' answer. Through the rectangular window beside me I could see the cloud had become very thick.

"Drop down below this weather, you won't see anything from up here." Now there was an impatient tone in Singleton's voice. From the other seat Chilton, who'd also been listening in, pulled a mocking gesture. I frowned my disapproval back at him.

The aircraft lurched down through the cloud and we came out slap bang over a town which Richards identified as Swindon, which meant we were a fair bit off the planned route. However, it gave him our position and he was able to turn back onto the correct course. An hour later we were back safe and sound in the briefing room at Heston.

"Navigation is an aviator's most important skill. Don't underestimate it." Singleton threw down his flying helmet and jacket. "That's enough for today. Let's have you back here first thing tomorrow morning." Richards left the room without saying a word and walked back to the Club House alone. When he didn't appear for dinner I went upstairs where I found him lying on his bed in shirtsleeves.

"Well, I really screwed that up, didn't I?" he muttered.

"Nonsense!" I tried to rally him. "You had bloody bad luck. That weather would have confused any pilot."

"Maybe," he sighed.

"You fancy a drink?"

"No thanks," He thumped the bed. "I need a clear head."

I remembered my conversation with Singleton about taking on the position of senior pilot and encouraging the others.

"Look, is there anything I can do to help?"

"No," he snapped back. Richards was a decent man, but it was obvious he lacked confidence in his own abilities and that could be fatal for a pilot. There was little I could do while he was in such a state of mind so I headed back downstairs.

The bar was quiet, behind the counter Pimm was thumbing through a copy of Picture Post magazine.

"Evening," she looked up and smiled.

"Anything interesting in there?" I nodded towards the magazine.

"Apparently, as there are no gala dances and few white tie dinner parties these days, us women are now wearing glamorous nightgowns to satisfy our passion for dressing up after dark."

"Is that so?"

"Yes, according to the article." She put down the magazine and I ordered a pint of bitter. "Where are your friends tonight?" she asked as she held up a glass to the light and checked it was clean.

"They're both getting early nights."

"That's a bit boring." She poured the pint and placed it in front of me. I took out my Dunhills.

"You got one of those for me?" she asked. I offered her the opened packet and she took a cigarette. She leant across the counter to catch the flame on the match that I had just struck. Her breasts pinched against the beer pumps.

"Have you worked here long?" I asked.

"Coming up to four years now." She delicately flicked

the first layer of ash into a tray. "Ron got the job of Airport Manager here in thirty-seven." I took it that Ron was her husband.

"So, he works here as well?"

"No, he's Royal Navy Reserve, so he got called up quickly. Right now he's out in the Mediterranean, somewhere." She took another drag and left a smudge of lipstick on the cigarette. "I only started working here when most of the lads got called up as well. We had about twenty staff at one point, now it's only me and Charlie out front, three in the kitchen and two chamber maids."

"Was it busy before the war?"

"At one point it was. They had big plans for the place." She surveyed the room as if she was remembering a better time. "It was going to be the main London airport, quite a few aircraft companies based themselves here, but it never really worked out. Lord knows what the future holds for us." She lifted a glass of red wine that she had hidden behind the counter and took a sip. "Where do you call home?" she asked.

"My family's from Oxford, but I've been pretty much nomadic for the past two years. Not sure where I'd call home now."

"Take a tip from me, don't settle down in some God forsaken boring place like this."

"Is it that bad here?"

"There's no bus, no trains, I can't even get to the pictures without a lift."

"Plenty of aircraft though."

"Yeah, if only I could fly!" She smirked and took

another sip of wine.

"If it's that boring I'll take you out one night." I said with a confidence that surprised me. She looked across the counter and our eyes met briefly.

"Careful, I might just take you up on that offer."

Our flirtations were suddenly cut short as two men arrived in the bar. She hid the glass of wine and quickly stubbed out her cigarette.

The men were both officers. The senior of the two was a Wing Commander with grey hair and glasses. I detected an Australian twang in his accent. The other was a younger Flight Lieutenant, with a lean clean shaven face. I recognised him as Rowbotham, the pilot who been flying the Spitfire that morning. They were engaged in a very intense conversation concerning the delivery of some camera equipment. I didn't take much notice of them, I was more interested in studying Pimm's figure as she moved about behind the bar. After a while the Wing Commander checked his watch, finished his drink and left. Rowbotham looked over towards me.

"I take it you're one of the new chaps?" he asked with a smile.

"Yes, I arrived yesterday."

"What was your last posting?"

"Fighters, down at Manston. Before that Hurricanes at North Weald."

"Really," he said raising an eyebrow. "Can I get you a drink?"

I gladly accepted his offer and Pimm refilled my glass.

"Sounds like you've got the right credentials for the job,"

he continued. "I don't think it will take you long to pass muster."

"How long have you been on this unit?" I asked.

"Since it was formed. It's been quite a challenge, but I think we're starting to prove our worth now. Although I'm not sure everyone's convinced of our potential."

"Oh, why's that?"

"Well, it's never been a conventional Air Force operation." He went on to tell me that the Unit had been secretly formed by an Australian businessman called Sydney Cotton. He was the Wing Commander who had just left the bar and the owner of the burgundy Rolls Royce. Cotton had been involved in aviation for many years. Just before the outbreak of war he proved to the Air Ministry how effective high speed photo reconnaissance aircraft could be by equipping his own Lockheed Electra with cameras and bringing back high quality aerial images of Germany. Ironically to do this he had used German made Leica cameras secretly mounted in the wingtips. The Air Ministry was impressed; Cotton was given a commission and the rank of Wing Commander. He assembled a team of engineers and pilots at Heston and under his supervision they modified a number of Spitfires for PR work.

They were very successful at first and Cotton was effectively given free rein to develop the unit. At this point they were jokingly referred to as Cotton's Private Air Force. However, the Air Ministry felt they needed more control over this important asset and Cotton's flamboyant enterprising spirit didn't fit well within their bureaucratic framework. As a consequence he was moved into an advisory role, although he still had a strong influence over the Unit.

"There's no doubt about it. We're going to be a very valuable part of the war effort. You've joined us at an important time." Rowbotham offered me a cigarette and flicked open a brass lighter. "Mark my words, whoever has the best intelligence will win this war."

"How dangerous are the operations?" I asked bluntly. He dragged on the cigarette and thought for a moment.

"It varies from job to job. When you're up high there's nowhere really to hide, but you've got the advantage of altitude." He raised his hand as if it was an aircraft and then lowered it down to the bar and twisted it around his glass. "If you're down low, you're harder to detect, but then if anything goes wrong you'll hit the deck before you know it." He let his hand fall to the countertop. "Personally, I always feel vulnerable flying anywhere between five hundred and eight thousand feet, but if you keep your wits about you you'll be okay." He looked at me with a dead pan expression. "Of course, the greatest danger is always engine failure, especially if you're deep behind the lines. So, keep an eye on those temperatures and pressures." I winced at the thought of having to force land in the middle of Bavaria. No way of escaping from there.

# Chapter 6

## Pass muster

We spent the following days planning and flying another round of navigation exercises. The PR unit alongside was always busy and we'd often see either Rowbotham or one of the other pilots disappear off in a Spitfire and return several hours later. I watched them with interest and a swell of frustration. Although I was happy to be active, I found parts of the training pretty mundane. Singleton, being ever astute, noticed this and at the end of the week had evidently decided to challenge my abilities.

The two of us flew down to Cornwall in the Oxford. We refuelled at St Mawgan on the north coast. From there Singleton planned a route which took us out over the Atlantic into a series of precise square patterns before coming back in over land. The weather was patchy and navigating over the ocean with no landmarks was difficult, but I made it back over the coast about a mile to the east of where I needed to be. By no means perfect, but close enough for me to correct the course.

Over Devon I picked up the River Ex and, although I was a minute and a half late, I managed to find the isolated village which had been set as my target. For this exercise I flew as the pilot in command in the left hand seat. Singleton said very little during the three hour flight. He sat with his arms folded carefully scrutinising my every action. It was hard work and there was no way of hiding any of my errors. By the time we arrived back at Heston I was exhausted.

"Good stuff." Singleton unstrapped himself. "Let's go and have a smoke."

We climbed out and walked over towards the briefing room. When we were clear of the aircraft he dropped his parachute to the floor and stretched his arms out. From his pocket he pulled out his pipe and a pouch of black tobacco. I found my Dunhills and lit one.

"I'm not one to be too complimentary and I don't like to embarrass people, but your flying ability is excellent." I couldn't help but smile at his comment. "However, you need to be careful with your navigation. You were out by a fair few points when you came over the coast. That's because you were looking for your waypoint far too early. It's a common problem, you must always remember to keep your eyes on the instruments until you're almost on top of the visual waypoint, otherwise, you'll drift."

The smile on my face wilted, I thought my navigation hadn't been that bad. Singleton clamped the pipe between his teeth and puffed on the lit tobacco. "Next week I want you to get as many hours in on the Spitfires as you can," he spoke through the corner of his mouth. "Start tomorrow morning if the weather holds, then you can take the weekend off. You've earned a couple of beers tonight, but I want to see you in church on Sunday morning."

"Which church would that be, sir?"

"Anyone with a God that's prepared to listen to you. That means if you ever get lost in the air, you've got someone to talk to." He laughed and walked away leaving a trail of smoke hanging on the late afternoon air.

I met Richards at dinner. He told me he had spent the day with Fenton recapping some basic navigation theory. I offered some words of encouragement, but he was very melancholy. He asked about my day, but I decided to refrain from telling him about my own progress and moved the conversation on.

Afterwards I phoned through from reception and asked for the meteorological forecast for the following day. A front was heading up from the Atlantic and it was likely that the best weather would be in the morning. I ordered an early breakfast from the kitchen and rationed myself to a single beer. I wanted a sober head for the following day.

The dawn came damp and cold. I arrived at the hangar to find Morgan waiting with his clipboard. On the edge of the airfield one of his precious Spitfires sat waiting. A thin band of daylight had cracked across the inky black sky and was gently outlining the edges of the aircraft.

I wandered around, casually checking that the tyres were inflated correctly, that the control surfaces were free from obstruction and all the maintenance panels were securely fastened.

"She's full of fuel and ready to go. Please don't bend her." Morgan handed me the 'Form 700', an official piece of paper, that declared that I was taking charge of the Spitfire. I signed it and one of the erks placed a parachute in the cockpit for me. I reached over and checked the straps. Morgan eyed me suspiciously as if I didn't trust his crew.

"Sorry, I won't take chances with a parachute." I explained. "I had to use one once and I always check they've been packed properly." I tucked a map and chinagraph pencil into the top of my left boot then wrapped my scarf around my neck and zipped up my Irvin jacket.

The Spitfire had a narrow fuselage and to make access easier there was a handy door which flapped down. I swung myself into the cockpit and sat down on the parachute pack. Morgan climbed up after me and by standing on the wing reached in and helped me buckle up the straps. I pulled on my leather flying helmet, plugged in the headset and connected the oxygen supply. Morgan slammed the door shut.

"Good luck," he muttered. I felt the aircraft bounce as he jumped off the wing. By now it was daylight and I was keen to get airborne.

In front were the controls, switches and instruments which had become so familiar to me. Using my left hand, I set the mixture control lever to rich and the engine throttle open by an inch. I checked the propeller pitch was fine. The dial by my left knee told me I had good air pressure in the brakes. I checked the fuel quantities in each tank. With my right hand I worked the brass ki gas pump and primed the engine. I pulled the control column hard back between my legs.

Morgan was now standing by the port wingtip waiting for my signal. I looked out towards him and gave a thumbs up, he nodded in response. I pressed the round black starter button. With a low whine the big black propeller turned slowly. Then I flicked the two magneto switches and the engine erupted into life.

I let the revs settle and watched the oil pressure start to rise. I strained my neck and looked around outside as best I could. The aircraft appeared fine and the sky looked clear. I eased off the brake and with a gentle touch to the throttle the Spitfire started to roll forward.

I taxied down to the end of the runway and then using the rudder and brakes spun around to face the brisk wind that was coming from the southeast. One final check of the instruments; everything still looked good. I pushed the throttle forward and started to move quickly down the runway. Immediately, I could feel that the power of the engine was greater than anything I'd experienced before and the aircraft was already begging to become airborne. Tentatively I allowed the tail to rise and within an instant the wheels were off the ground. I was surprised by the liveliness of the aircraft and I was a little jerky with my movements on the stick. I retracted the undercarriage and climbed gently away from the airfield.

It was exhilarating to be back in a powerful machine after a week of flying the sedate little Oxford. I flew north for a few miles and then west. Within two minutes I was at six thousand feet and in a fine layer of wispy cloud. I now had plenty of altitude and I was eager to see how she handled, so I decided to perform some aerobatics. I pulled the stick back firmly into a climb and then eased it to the right. The world spun around me in a lazy barrel roll. Then I pushed forward, gathered speed and pulled up sharply. I raced upwards until I was vertical and then let the aircraft tip over in a loop. She was fast and responsive exactly as Singleton had described. He was also right about the centre of gravity and it took me sometime to trim the controls.

I throttled forward again and held her in a steady climb. With the rate of climb being four times quicker than the Oxford it wasn't long before I was levelling out at twenty thousand feet. Now the earth far below me was completely obscured by clouds. Once again I checked the engine instruments; everything was still looking good so I started to climb once more until I was nearly at thirty thousand feet. This was the highest altitude I'd ever reached. I banked the port wing over and took in my surroundings. The atmosphere above was a deep blue and a ribbon of pale magenta light flooded over the cloudscape below. I flew on basking in the freedom of flight and the sunlight that shone through the canopy.

At that height the air was very thin and I noticed the engine performance had reduced. I let the nose drop and immediately started to pick up speed. I watched the needle on the air speed indicator start to rise. Very quickly I was approaching three hundred and twenty miles an hour, then three hundred and fifty, but before I reached three hundred and sixty I lost my nerve and levelled out. As thrilling as it was to fly so fast I was seriously worried that the aircraft could break up or I might not be able to pull out of the dive. I flew on and then started to descend again, this time at a shallower angle and slower speed.

At eight thousand feet I started to see the earth through patches of cloud. I was northwest of Reading and could see the town over to port. I took a wide descending curve around the outskirts and picked up the railway line which ran east towards London. Now I dropped down low and chased a steam train that was running out of the town. In only a few moments I'd gone from the roof of the world to skimming over the treetops.

I covered fifteen miles then climbed up and spotted Heston off of my starboard quarter. I flew high over the airfield to check the wind hadn't changed, then turned into the circuit and carefully slipped the aircraft down onto the ground. I taxied over and found Singleton was waiting for me at the hangar.

"Did you enjoy yourself?" he asked as I climbed out of the cockpit.

"Yes, she's bloody quick." I jumped down onto the soft grass.

"She takes a bit of getting used to. I'd relax your angle of descent slightly when you come in on your approach." As we stood there another gust of wind whipped around behind us and the aircraft rocked.

"I'll tell Morgan to get her inside," He looked up at the mass of cumulonimbus clouds which were heading towards us. "Looks like we've had the best of the weather."

Inside the crew room I found Chilton reading a newspaper.

"I see you've just been up in the Spit."

"Yes, managed to get in before the weather changed."

"I imagine it won't be long before I get to take her up myself." There was a hint of jealousy in his tone.

"Be careful when you do. She's quick to climb, but pretty

unforgiving on the ground." I found a mug and poured in some tea from a flask. "Where's Richards?"

"He's gone up with Fenton. They're doing another nav exercise."

I looked through the window, the white clouds were turning black and it looked as if the rain was about to start. I pitied Richards, a navigation exercise in this weather would be difficult.

"Have we got any more milk?" I asked, stirring the dark brown liquid in my mug with a tarnished teaspoon. Chilton shook his head.

"No sorry, I think I finished it off." I picked up the empty jug and headed over to see if I could scrounge some milk from the erks in the hangar.

As I walked between the buildings I heard the soft drone of engines in the distance. I looked over to the east and saw the dark shape of the Oxford approaching. By now the wind was much stronger and large spots of rain were hitting the concrete. I watched on knowing that these winds would make this a challenging landing for Richards. Even far off I could tell he was battling hard to keep the aircraft on track. I judged he was too high coming in over the airfield perimeter, but he had plenty of space to correct himself. He straightened his approach and seemed to have the aircraft under control when a sudden gust came rolling across. He overcorrected the rudder and throttled the engines back too quickly. The Oxford sagged onto the ground with a bump. The port wing flicked up and once again he overcorrected, the starboard wheel drove into the ground throwing up a spume of mud and the aircraft slewed round in a circle. The engines stopped and the aircraft came to a standstill facing the direction it had come from.

"Get a crash tender out now!" bellowed Morgan who had also been watching from the hangar. The door behind me burst open and Singleton ran out over the apron to see what had happened. I watched on with the empty milk jug in my hand as Fenton and Richards climbed out from the fuselage. They were obviously unhurt, but the aircraft had been badly damaged.

# Chapter 7

## High Sierra

That afternoon I drove the Bentley into Ealing. It was raining hard. The car had no windscreen wipers, so I had to drive slowly. I posted a letter home and a cheque to a fellow pilot at Manston who I still owed some money to. I hoped that my wages would clear my account before he banked the cheque. I also sent a telegram to Fanshaw asking if there had been any news on my greatcoat.

Back at Heston I found that Richards and all his belongings had gone from our room, I wasn't surprised. I felt sorry for him, he was a good man, but it was far better to make mistakes and find your limits in training rather than on an operation.

"So, poor old Dicky's gone," said Chilton when I caught up with him in the bar that evening. "Doesn't surprise me, he didn't have the right stuff."

"I'd be careful what you say." I slammed my pint down on the table, I'd had enough of his bullish attitude. "Until you've been tested I'd advise you to keep your lip buttoned. It was bloody windy out there today and anyone of us could have ended up like he did."

"Steady on," Chilton reeled back, but I'd lost my cool and carried on.

"Listen, when you've been out on an operation, flown through flak or had a 109 on your tail, come back here and you can tell me all about it. Hell, I'll even buy you drinks for the night, but until then shut up!" I braced myself expecting him to come back at me with either a verbal or physical assault. However, he just stared at me with a pathetic expression of bewilderment and an awkward silence filled the void between us.

"I'm sorry," I apologised feeling a little calmer. "Richards may not have been the best pilot, but he doesn't deserve to be run down."

"Yes, quite so," he muttered. "Can I get you another drink?" he asked gingerly. I accepted and we drew a line under our altercation. It was good to clear the air and tell him what I thought of his attitude, but now that was over and we needed to move on. Rowbotham and a few of the other pilots were in the bar that evening and with no flying scheduled for the following day we held a very rowdy darts tournament.

The next day I woke up in an uncomfortably quiet atmosphere. It had only been a week but I'd got used to sharing the room with Richards and it seemed odd without him. I lay under the covers with no great ambition to get out of bed until boredom overcame me.

I got up, drew back the curtains and opened the window. The weather was still foul, but the air was fresh on my face. Somewhere in the distance a peal of church bells was calling parishioners to Sunday worship.

I took a bath in six inches of tepid water and shivered my way back down the corridor. I'd missed breakfast by a wide margin but managed to scrounge a toasted crumpet from Charlie. Then I found a discarded copy of the Times in the lounge and attacked the crossword.

"Busy morning?" Pimm was walking through with a tray of cups.

"Hardly," I said with a mouth full of crumpet. I watched her walk past into the kitchen, she was wearing a dark blue dress that was slightly too tight for her and I could just make out the shape of her underwear. I went back to the crossword and tried to remember which perennial plants began with the letter F. A moment later the kitchen door swung open and she appeared again.

"You going to keep your promise then?"

"Which one was that?"

"You taking me to the pictures," she spoke in a hushed tone, although the lounge was empty. "I finish at three. We can make the four o'clock showing."

I was surprised by her forwardness, but seeing as I had nothing else planned for the afternoon I thought I'd humour her.

"Okay, I'll meet you at three then."

"Pick me up from behind the kitchen. This might be a dull place but tongues still wag." She walked off and I took the opportunity to study her figure again.

At four o'clock we were tucked away in the back row of the Empire cinema on Ealing Broadway. The fog of cigarette smoke mixed with the steam of wet raincoats rose up over the stalls and caught the beam of the film projector.

We sat through the newsreels and watched footage of Winston Churchill inspecting Czechoslovakian troops. Then the audience settled as the main feature started - High Sierra, the story of a robbery that went wrong. Humphrey Bogart mooched around the screen with his collar undone and tie loosened. He reminded me of Fanshaw.

Halfway through the feature I felt Pimm nuzzle her shoulder against me and her hand clasped hold of my arm.

"It's cold in here," she whispered. There was an exciting comfort in feeling her close to me and the scent of her perfume again. When we arrived back at the Club House I followed her up the stairs, she didn't stop me. She lived at the far end of the first floor in the Manager's suite of rooms. She took a key from her purse and with her scarlet tipped fingers turned the lock. Once we were inside she pushed the door shut behind me and dropped the latch.

"Now, you need to understand. This is all a bit of fun and nothing else," she spoke softly as she undid the buttons on my tunic. I had never spent a Sunday afternoon quite like that one. The rain pounded hard against the window and a photograph of her husband stared at me from the dressing table.

"Don't worry about him," she said afterwards as we lay naked on the bed. "No doubt he'll be enjoying himself with some Maltese whore."

"When did you last see him?"

"Two years ago, we had an argument on the night he left for Malta and we never made up. He sends money and a letter once a month. I can't say I'm looking forward to him coming back. With any luck he'll get torpedoed."

"That's a bit cruel."

"Take my advice, go have some fun. Don't get married." She turned to look at me. "Not yet anyway, you're too young."

"I can't get married, I've not found the right girl yet." I reached over to touch her thigh, but she moved away off of the bed and stood up. She walked over to the dressing table and started to adjust her hair in the mirror. The light from the table lamp caught the curve of her back and projected a shapely silhouette on the wall behind.

"While you're here you can come and see me again, but remember it's only a bit of fun." A bit of fun was all that I'd hoped for, but she aroused in me a desire to be close to someone. I would have happily laid in the bed all night with her alongside me, however she was having none of it. I was sent back to my room and had to tiptoe through the corridors in bare feet.

I slept well that night and bounced down to breakfast the next morning. The weather front had moved and an area of high pressure had brought some sunshine. Outside a gentle breeze carried a faint promise of spring. In the briefing room Fenton gave me a target to photograph in the Spitfire.

"Here you go," he scrawled a circle in red chinagraph around Milford Haven. "Plan your route accordingly and let's see what you bring back."

I took off at ten, flew a course west over the Bristol Channel and was back at Heston in time for lunch. The photographs I'd taken were removed from the camera and developed. Later that afternoon Fenton came in and handed me three black and white prints which showed a crystal clear image of the Welsh town.

"They're okay, but the weather was in your favour today." I think that was the nearest Fenton could get to giving a compliment. "You'll have a similar exercise tomorrow."

I spent the next five days flying as much as I could. Later in the week the rain returned and I had a bad time trying to find Grantham in thick cloud. Running low on fuel I found another airfield which turned out to be a bomber station and after a few administrative issues managed to get my tanks refilled.

By Friday I had a portfolio full of photographs and had logged eight hours on the Spitfire. Chilton also worked hard that week and successfully flew a solo exercise himself. It was obvious that his arrogance had been a compensation for his own lack of confidence. Once he overcame this, his attitude rapidly improved and he started to prove himself as a capable pilot.

That evening Singleton joined Rowbotham, Chilton and me in the mess.

"Here's to a good week's work." Singleton raised his whisky glass. "I don't want to talk shop at the bar, but it won't be long before you're both operational."

"Any idea on our postings?" asked Chilton. It was a naive question, no pilot, sailor or soldier ever knew where he was going to be sent next.

"No, haven't got a clue, but we'll find somewhere for you."

"Somewhere warm please," I joked.

"Careful what you wish for," warned Singleton. "You don't want to end up in some mosquito-infested desert. I got stuck for two weeks in Juba which was pretty nasty."

It suddenly occurred to me why Singleton appeared familiar to me. He had been a pilot in the African Air Race which ran from England to Johannesburg. It was a harrowing six thousand mile route which claimed the lives of several men and out of the fourteen aircraft which entered only one made it to the finish line. As a teenager I'd followed the story in the newspapers and that's where I'd seen Singleton's picture. I listened keenly as he went on to regale us with stories about his air racing days and some of the exotic places he flown through.

At the bar Pimm caught my arm. For fear of embarrassment, mine more than hers, I'd not spoken to her since our tryst.

"You don't have to avoid me," she whispered.

"I wasn't trying to," I lied.

"I see there's a new film out on Saturday. Fancy taking me out again?" I became aware that Rowbotham was watching me, his eye caught mine and he gave me a subtle wink. I looked away in embarrassment and felt a surge of blood rush to my cheeks.

"Eh … I'm not sure if I'm flying over the weekend," I stammered.

"Well, if you're not, pick me up at six tomorrow." She pushed through the crush of people and collected some empty glasses.

"Looks like you've been operational already," Rowbotham gave a hearty laugh and slapped me on the back.

"Sorry, what do you mean?" I made a poor attempt at acting innocent.

"I wouldn't worry, you're not the first. She collects young pilots like schoolboys collect stamps. I bet she taught you a thing or two." My cheeks were burning now. I felt as if I'd been caught cheating at cards and had no defence. I left the bar and hid in the toilets for a full ten minutes.

In the end I managed to overcome my humiliation and encouraged by a physical urge I took Pimm out on the following day. However, the excitement and spark that was there the week before was hard to reignite. It was past midnight when I returned to my own room feeling shameful and slightly disappointed.

Chilton and I commenced the following week with more flying on the Spitfires. Then on the Wednesday afternoon Fenton called me into the little office alongside the operations room.

"You wanted to see me sir?" I asked.

"Yes, we have been asked to supply an aircraft and pilot for operational duty immediately. The Boss and I have agreed to send you." I was excited by the news, but somewhat apprehensive. "I was hesitant to send you at first. I know you've got combat experience, but I'd like to see you with more hours on photo ops. However, the Boss has put his foot down." There was a hint of resignation in his voice.

"Where's the posting sir?" I was desperate to know.

"I gather you wanted somewhere hot?" I nodded. "Well, hard luck you're going to Wick in Scotland." He stood up and walked over to a small scale chart of the British Isles which was pinned to the wall. Using a pencil he pointed to the northeast tip of Scotland.

"Blimey, how far away is that?"

"As the crow flies, about five hundred miles. I suggest you plan your route this evening and get airborne at first light tomorrow."

"How long am I likely to be there?"

"For the foreseeable future. You'll have to leave your car here and anything that you can't squeeze into the cockpit. There's a PR unit already set up there, but they lost their pilot and aircraft yesterday." I didn't like the sound of that.

"How was he lost?"

"I don't know, but he needs to be replaced immediately. You'll report directly to Flight Lieutenant Lamont who will be your Flight Commander. There's an Intelligence Officer by the name of Prowse who will give you the briefings for each job. It's all written down here." He pushed over a handwritten note with the details. I looked back up at the chart and squinted at the small pencil mark he had made. I wondered what this small remote Scottish town would be like.

Early the next morning I drove the Bentley down to the hangar and left it with Morgan.

"Don't worry, I'll make sure the lads look after it." He sniffed the air and smelt the exhaust fumes. "It's running a little rich, I'll get that adjusted for you."

There was a deep rumbling as the huge rolling doors on the hangar were pulled open and the Spitfire that I was to fly was pushed out.

"I've given her a look over myself," said Morgan. "When you get to Scotland make sure they take good care of it."

He helped me stow my kit behind the cockpit. There wasn't much room between the camera gear and I'd had to leave some of my belongings with Charlie at the Club House. I'd just finished checking over the aircraft myself when Singleton pulled up in his Rover.

"All set?" His keen eyes darted over the aircraft behind me.

"I think so, sir."

"It should be a straightforward flight for you. Just keep a bloody good look out for any high ground and mountains." He reached into the glove box of his car and took something out. "Here, take this." He handed me a small rectangular box. I opened it, inside was a wristwatch. It had a large black face with a chrome surround and was set on a thick leather strap.

"Remember, good navigation requires good time keeping. That's Swiss made, very accurate," he explained. "It belonged to an old pal of mine, he won't need it now and I've already got one. I'd rather see it being used than collecting dust in my desk drawer."

"Thank you." I was stunned by his generosity, it was a far better time piece than the watch I'd been issued with. I was wise enough not to ask what had happened to his friend.

Morgan helped me up into the cockpit and gave an affectionate slap on my shoulder as he stepped down. After three weeks at Heston I'd just about won his respect. I looked over towards the Club House and wondered if

Pimm would miss me or just forget me. The latter most likely.

I started the engine and taxied out. Singleton was leaning against his car with one foot on the running board. He was watching me carefully with an almost paternal anxiety.

I took off and turned onto a course which took me up the east coast of England. Forty minutes later I landed at Brieghton, just south of York. I had the fuel tanks refilled, stretched my legs and then pressed on to Scotland.

The landscape changed dramatically as I flew north. I passed over lush green farmland, thick woodland, sandy heathland and grey towns. The terrain rose and fell like a creased bedsheet. Just north of the border I hit bad weather which engulfed the coastline all the way to Inverness. I climbed up above the clouds until it eventually cleared over the Moray Firth. As I checked the map I realised that this was the furthest north I'd ever been.

From there on, the airfield was fairly easy to locate. It lay north of Wick Bay about a mile in land. Its defining feature was a long concrete runway which ran at right angles to the coast. Landing on concrete was going to be a novelty for me. All the airfields I'd flown from had grass runways, but Wick was built to accommodate larger aircraft which could easily sink into the soft Scottish peat.

I was anxious to touch down smartly as there was every chance that my new colleagues would be watching and critiquing my landing. However, as I came into the final approach I felt a crosswind push the aircraft to one side. I'd often landed in crosswinds, with a big wide open grass airfield it didn't matter if you came in slightly to the side, but on a concrete runway you had to touch down right on the centre line. As a result, I struggled to line up and came down slightly too hard, the concrete surface snatched at the tyres and I bounced. It was a messy landing which frustrated me beyond measure, but I was down safely.

I taxied over towards a hangar and killed the engine. I was surprised by the atmosphere when I slid back the canopy. It was warmer than I'd expected it to be and the hazy sunlight cast a serene hue over the horizon. Where the bloody hell had that crosswind gone?

# Chapter 8

## Wick

"What's your business here?" Came a shrill shout from a truck that had just pulled up alongside my Spitfire. Leaning out of the cab was an officer with thick eyebrows and an agitated scowl.

"I'm looking for the photo reconnaissance unit."

"That's the other side of the hangars. You should have known that." It wasn't the friendliest of welcomes. The officer turned and shouted to a group of erks who were standing by a small tractor. "Get that aircraft out of my way now!" The erks came over and started to hitch up the tractor to the tail wheel of the Spitfire.

While I waited I took in my surroundings. Wick was primarily a Coastal Command station, meaning that the squadrons based here would be mainly operating over the sea on duties such as convoy protection and attacks on enemy shipping.

I noticed two Armstrong Whitworth Whitleys being prepared for flight. The Whitley was a large twin engine aircraft with a gangly narrow fuselage that jutted forward at the front like an over pronounced chin. I had a fondness for the type as before the war I'd been an apprentice at Armstrong Whitworth and had spent a good deal of time making brackets for the engines. There appeared to be another squadron at Wick as well. They were equipped with the Lockheed Hudson. Like the Whitleys these had twin engines but were smaller and far more rugged. They were American aircraft that had been purchased before the war. I thought back to Fanshaw's comments about us getting into too much debt with the United States.

"All set sir," shouted the tractor driver as the engine coughed up a puff of black smoke. With one man at each wingtip and me following behind, we walked over the airfield like a cortège at some funeral procession.

On the northside of the main hangars were three semi-cylindrical Nissen huts. These corrugated iron buildings were a common site on RAF stations and were used for everything from barracks to workshops. They came in different sizes and various states of repair. These were brand-new, the concrete around the footings was still green. On the nearest hut a small hand painted sign on the side of the door held the letters PRU.

The tractor came to a stop and the erks set about unhitching the aircraft. I retrieved my kitbag from the fuselage and walked over towards the huts.

"Hello!" called a man hanging out of an open window. "You're Sommers aren't you?"

"Yes,"

"Cracking! You're just in time for coffee. Come inside."

The Nissen hut was divided into different sections, the first being the crew room. It was an untidy space with bundles of flying equipment spread around and piles of magazines stacked on a low table. I walked in and added my kit bag to the mess.

"I'm Lamont by the way, the chaps call me Larry," said the man. He was a stocky figure with a receding hair line and low Yorkshire growl. "Thank the lord, they've sent us someone with some experience." He pulled my flying jacket open and pressed my medal ribbon. "I was worried they would send some spotty boy scout." He handed me an enamel mug and filled it from a pot that was bubbling on a metal stove. "How was the flight up?" Lamont asked as he poured a mug for himself.

"I had to climb up over a bit of cloud, but apart from that it was a good run."

"I saw the runway caught you out a little." I winced with embarrassment, he had obviously seen my landing.

"Yes, the surface snatched the tyres." I pleaded my case.

"Don't worry, these concrete runways take a bit of getting used to." He smiled. "They are wonderful for bad weather, but much harder on the undercarriage than the grass strips."

We sat down in two wicker chairs and he went on to explain how the unit was set up. It was all fairly new and he had only been promoted to the rank of Flight Lieutenant in the last week. Including me there would now be three pilots and two Spitfires. Officially we reported to the Station Commander, but Lamont said they rarely saw him.

"How busy does it get here?" I asked.

"It can vary." He stirred a spoonful of sugar into his coffee. "As you might have guessed, from up here we mainly cover Norway and a bit of Denmark. Strategically the area is useful for the German Navy, it's much easier for them to sail out into the North Atlantic from Norway rather than through the English Channel. There's also a lot of deep water around the Fjords where they like to hide battleships and harbours they can use for U-boats."

I heard one of the Whitley's start its engines. I looked out of the window and saw the aircraft starting to edge forward. The clouds had parted and were allowing the sun to shine through briefly.

"It's warmer up here than I'd imagined,"

"Aye, we get two types of weather, dead calm or blowing a bloody gale, and it switches between the two without warning."

When we'd finished coffee, Lamont showed me around the rest of the unit. In the first Nissen hut was the crew room and an office which doubled as an operations room.

"We report here every morning and wait for orders," he explained. In the office was a plump female corporal with an enormous bosom. Her name was Berthon and she was affectionately known to the pilots as Bertha.

"She's one of the most efficient admin clerks you'll ever meet," said Lamont. "She can punch the keys on an Imperial typewriter quicker than you can fire bullets from a Vickers machine gun."

The other two huts alongside housed a darkroom for processing films and a photographic interpretation room. Lamont knocked on the darkroom door and opened it. Inside, a man was washing and hanging black and white prints on a string line. He squinted as daylight flooded in from the open door. It was a gloomy place with black walls, trays of chemicals and a pungent smell which pinched my sinuses. Three photographic enlargers were lined up on a bench and a great wooden drum for drying films hung from the ceiling.

Next door the interpretation room was far more bright and cheerful. The curved walls were painted white and two large map tables had been pushed together in the centre of the room. At the far end of the hut was a series of neatly labelled filing cabinets and chests. Around the table was a cluster of people, two men were placing negatives into large envelopes and a woman was filling out index cards. In the centre was a female officer studying a photograph with a strange contraption that looked like a microscope, over her shoulder a man was watching her. He too was an officer, a middle-aged Flight Lieutenant with thin white hair and a moustache. He shot a hard look at Lamont as if to question the reason for the intrusion.

"This is Sommers, the new boy," Lamont explained. "I'm giving him the tour. This is Flight Lieutenant Prowse, he coordinates the operations and scrutinises our hard work." The female officer looked up from the photograph. She was an attractive woman with a round pretty face, blonde hair and an instantly disarming smile.

"Hello," I said pathetically. Prowse raised an irritated eyebrow.

"Best leave them to it," Lamont suggested quietly. We stepped outside and started walking back to the crew room. "I'm afraid Prowse is a bit of an old curmudgeon. The girls called him the Lobster."

"Why?"

"It's because he has a habit of picking up documents and photographs with his thumb and forefinger, like a claw." Lamont demonstrated with his own hand.

Suddenly, out of nowhere a Spitfire roared low overhead. It pulled up over the airfield and waggled its wings.

"That's Kalman back from a sortie." Lamont glanced at his watch. "He's later than I'd expected." It was common that a pilot would buzz the airfield when returning from an operation. It would wake everyone up and let them know he was intending to land. Two men came racing out from the interpretation room behind us.

The Spitfire turned hard and I could see the undercarriage start to lower. This pilot was obviously familiar with landing on the hard surface and, unlike my untidy effort, he touched down gently. The two men were eagerly waiting for the aircraft at the edge of the concrete apron, presently they were joined by Prowse. I watched as the pilot taxied quickly towards us, weaving the Spitfire left and right so he could see where he was going. He slowed down and almost came to a stop before giving a short burst of throttle to turn the aircraft into wind, throwing up a cloud of dust and gravel as he did so. The two men leapt forward and were unbuttoning the access panels before the propeller had stopped turning. One of them took the film magazines from the cameras and ran back towards the darkroom, while the other was left to refix the panels. The cockpit door fell open and the thin figure of the pilot threw off the shoulder straps and climbed out.

"Why are you late?" Prowse questioned him curtly.

"Cloud over the target sir, I had to wait for it to clear."

"Very well, I'll speak to you inside." Prowse walked away with a quick stride and short uptight steps. Kalman jumped down from the wing.

"How was it Johnny?" asked Lamont.

"Okay, apart from the weather." Kalman took off his helmet and pushed his blonde forelock back into place. He was a sergeant pilot with a young face, but serious expression. He put his head down and followed Prowse into the interpretation hut.

Later that day I had a demonstration of how erratic the weather around Wick could be. With no immediate orders Lamont and I were sitting outside the crew room lazing in the early spring sunshine.

"That looks ominous," he was staring at a bank of cumulus clouds creeping in slowly from the north. Within fifteen minutes the sky had darkened, five minutes later a heavy downpour forced us to shelter inside.

"So, you play any sports?" Lamont asked as we watched the rain pelting the ground.

"Cricket mainly."

"Play any rugger?"

"Not much." I felt his eyes assessing my physique.

"Pity, I'm trying to get a scratch side up to take on the Navy boys down the road. We've got plenty of weight in the forwards but I need some good hands out on the wing."

Having a slight frame and recently broken elbow the idea of playing rugby didn't appeal to me.

"Oh, I'd be no good." I said in my most feeble voice.

Beyond the runway a small white light flickered in the

cloud. I watched in amazement as one of the Lockheed Hudson's valiantly fought its way through the weather. The visibility across the airfield was appalling, I could barely see the far side of the hangars, but somehow the pilot managed to place it down safely on the centre line.

"They're made of stern stuff those Coastal Command chaps," remarked Lamont. "It was weather like this that did for Hamilton last week." I assumed Hamilton was the pilot I was replacing.

"What happened to him?"

"He was lost in low cloud and flew slap bang into the side of Mount Morven." Flying into high ground was a danger that had claimed many lives and it worried me greatly. I'd been lost in cloud before, but that was when I'd been flying over low and flat ground. There were lots of mountains and hills up here and of course in Norway there were many more. A wave of anxiety washed over me as I considered what dangers I might be facing in the very near future, flying up here was going to be a challenge.

That afternoon I booked into the Officers' Mess and when the bar opened at six o'clock I was the stewards first customer. It was a relief to be back on a functioning RAF station. The accommodation at Heston had been very comfortable, but I'd found the atmosphere uneasy. It was strange to be working in a strict disciplined environment and at the same time living in a luxury hotel. I also found it awkward with so many civilians around the airfield, without a uniform or rank one never really knew who you were speaking to. It put me on edge and I could never relax properly. At Wick there was a lot less comfort, but I knew where I was and who I was talking to.

Over the following days I familiarised myself with the local area. I logged as many airborne hours as I could, but with only two aircraft the opportunities were limited. Lamont gave me as much help as he could and pointed out a couple of useful landmarks.

"If you get lost one of the best ways to get back is to fly down the coastline. Although there are several lighthouses which all look similar, so don't get confused," he warned. "The nearest to us is the Noss Head which is slightly northeast of the airfield. There's the wreck of an old boat on the beach just north of here, that's always good for a fix. Inland it's much more difficult, a lot of the hills look the same, but they do have different colours. I suppose it's down to the heather that grows on the slopes. If you do get stuck in land strike a bearing northeast and you'll pop out on the coast somewhere. Oh, and one thing you must know is that they've built an entire fake runway in the moss about two miles north of here. The station has been bombed a few times and the idea is to confuse the enemy. It's very convincing, but whatever you do don't try landing on it!"

# Chapter 9

## Norway from twenty thousand feet

I was sitting in the crew room lamenting the last of my Dunhill cigarettes. The tobacconist in Wick was poorly stocked and I'd been forced to buy a carton of Woodbines. Lamont was lying sideways across a chair and throwing an old leather rugby ball up and down. Kalman was opposite me, his head obscured by a thick book.

"You're not thinking of starting a revolution are you?" asked Lamont. I looked over and read the cover of Kalman's tome: 'A Critique of Political Economy'.

"Just because I'm reading Marx doesn't make me a communist." Kalman spoke without lowering the pages. "Socialism is what I believe in."

"And just what's that when it's at home?"

"There are many facets," Kalman sighed like an irritated parent and put down the book. "Essentially I believe we should nationalise our industries and put more power into the hands of the masses."

"Sounds like Bolshevism to me," Lamont said throwing the ball higher. Kalman looked towards me.

"This war is going to end one day and we'll have a

chance to rebuild our society for the better."

"We'd better make sure we win then." I quipped.
Kalman shook his head and returned to his book.

A moment later Bertha appeared with a message and I
was summoned to see Prowse. I poured myself a mug of
coffee and walked over to the interpretation hut.

"You wanted to see me?" I asked standing in the
doorway of his office. Prowse cocked his head to one side
and stared at me.

"It is customary to salute," he muttered. I suppose he
was correct, he was senior to me, but very rarely did anyone
bother with those formalities on an operational unit.
Although I knew that discipline and respect were crucial to
the effective running of any military organisation, I'd
become quite cynical about those senior to me who had
never faced the enemy or proved themselves as aviators.

"Sorry, I left my cap in the crew room." As per King's
regulations I should have only saluted when wearing
headdress. "Shall I go back and get it?"

"No!" he snapped. "Just come in." I stepped into the
room and closed the door behind me.

"Now, Lamont maybe your Flight Commander here, but
regarding operations I give the damn orders. Understand?"

"Yes," I thought I'd better not strain his temper any
further.

"I've got a job for you to do this afternoon."

"Sounds interesting ……Sir."

"The targets are straightforward. We need pictures of
Bergen. Specifically, the west side of the port. We are
suspicious about the building works that are being

undertaken there. I want two passes over the port from twenty thousand feet. Then I want you to proceed to Måløy. It's a town about one hundred miles north of Bergen. Again, I want two passes of the target at twenty thousand feet." He produced a document with the operational details neatly typed out.

"Any questions?"

"I don't think so,"

"Good, get airborne as soon as you can."

He held the paper between his clawlike fingers and I couldn't help noticing that his hands also had a blotchy red complexion like the shell of a Lobster. I took the details back to the operations room and set about planning the trip. From a chest of drawers Bertha found the charts I needed.

"This is the latest information we've got," she said as she laid them across the desk. I studied the charts, everything about Norway seemed rugged, from the jagged coastlines to the sound of the place names. I found Bergen easy enough, the well sheltered port on the west coast. Måløy was a little more difficult to locate, it was a much smaller fishing port on an island to the north.

"What are these?" I pointed to some handmade annotations on the chart. Bertha leant her ample frame across the desk.

"Those are air defences that haven't been officially marked up yet." With a pencil she picked out a red circle and the letters AA. "That's a flak battery that was reported last week." Then she pointed to a red X and the word fighter. "And that's an active fighter airfield."

"Fighters?" I asked with some surprise.

"Yes, most probably 109s."

The flak battery was far enough away for me not to worry about, but I didn't like the idea of being that close to a fighter airfield. It was only about fifteen miles from Bergen. I read the orders that Prowse had given me again. They stated that I was to fly to Bergen first and then Måløy afterwards. If I flew directly to Bergen I'd probably be detected as I crossed the coastline. From there it would take me two minutes to reach the target, then I would have to spend three minutes making the two passes. All in all, that was five minutes, not enough time for a 109 to be scrambled from the ground and climb to my altitude. However, if one was already airborne at anywhere near eight thousand feet, it could easily reach me. If I then turned north he could make a very good interception from my port quarter with the sun behind him. I drummed on the table with a pencil and sighed, Bertha gave me a look of concern.

"Have we got the met reports for today?" I asked her.

"No not yet, I'll go and chase them up." She left the room.

I looked back over the charts, I wasn't keen to put myself at such a risk, especially as it was my first operation on the unit. I decided to fly the course in reverse. There was much less chance of being detected if I flew to Måløy first, then headed south to Bergen. If they tried to intercept me this way I would have a clear run home with the advantage of the sun being in their eyes. Prowse would be none the wiser and if I got the results who cared.

I took a ruler and pencil and started to plan the route. I made a careful note of what time I should reach the Norwegian Coast and the landmarks to look for. My major concern was the three hundred and sixty miles of North Sea I had to cross first. I'd never had to fly over such a large area of water before. With no landmarks, if I drifted slightly I could miss the target completely.

Bertha returned with the meteorological reports that suggested clear skies over the target, although at Wick it was currently gloomy and grey. I decided it was best to get going as soon as possible, if I was airborne at thirteen hundred I should be over Måløy two hours later.

I had a corned beef sandwich brought over to the crew room, but I could only stomach half of the wretched thing as my stomach muscles had tightened. I rummaged around in my jacket and found my hip flask. It was silver with a glass body and leather shoulders. It had been a gift from a dear friend and I used it probably more than I should have. I unscrewed the lid and took a sip of the whisky inside. I felt my nerves steady and my insides tingled. My God it felt good to be operational again, the weeks of training and sitting around had finally come to an end.

I checked over the Spitfire and tested the camera system was working. One of the erks ran the engine up while I strapped on my parachute. I climbed in, made myself comfortable and swung the aircraft around towards the runway. At thirteen-o-two I was airborne and climbing out over the North Sea on a direct heading for Norway.

At twenty thousand feet I levelled out and settled on the course. For the next hour the landscape of brilliant white

114

cloud rolled away beneath me. There was little else to do but check the instruments and listen to the drone of the Merlin engine. Then about one hundred and fifty miles from the coast the cloud thinned and I caught sight of the North Sea glistening in the afternoon sun. From that altitude the great body of water appeared to have a reddish brown hue. It looked tranquil, although I could just make out the white tops of some strong waves. Off to the north I spotted two ships, I presumed they were battleships although I couldn't make out any details. I made a note of their positions on the off chance the information was important to someone.

Then, in the distance the grey mass of the Norwegian coast came into view. I spotted my first landmark, a lighthouse at the foot of a steep mountain. I was a few degrees off course, but well within tolerance. I found Måløy tucked around the mouth of a fjord. I flew a wide turn around the area, just to make sure no one was creeping up on me, and then straightened up for my run across the target. I flicked the switch to operate the camera and hoped that everything was working. I made the second pass and then struck a course south towards Bergen.

Now an uncomfortable feeling of vulnerability started to grow over me. If I'd been detected, which was highly likely, a fighter may have been dispatched to intercept me. I pushed the throttle forward and picked up speed. I ignored the impressive landscape below with its craggy grey rocks and white snowcapped peaks, although a thought crossed my mind that I had no provisions for surviving in such a harsh environment if I found myself down there.

Bergen appeared off my starboard wing. I looked down at the busy port and lined up into my target run. Flying straight and level over enemy territory contradicted all my instincts as a fighter pilot. If anyone was behind me there was no way of knowing, I'd have been easy pickings. By the time I finished my second run my heart was racing and I was drenched in sweat. Satisfied that I'd completed the task I broke away and pushed the throttle forward again.

Ten minutes later I was out over the North Sea with a belly full of photographs. Everything had gone to plan so I settled down for the long run home. I trimmed the flying controls and set the engine to a comfortable cruising speed. I was confident in my navigation, but as a precaution when I was halfway over the sea I asked for a radio fix. I was delighted to find I was only slightly off course by a few degrees. I touched down at Wick in the early evening. The erks retrieved the films and I pulled myself out of the cockpit.

"How was it?" Lamont asked. He had come out to watch my arrival with Prowse.

"All good, clear run over both targets." I climbed down and unzipped my jacket.

"Anything else to report?" asked Prowse.

"I did spot a couple of battleships."

"Fill that in and give the locations of the ships you saw." He tore a sheet of paper from a pad and handed it to me. It was a combat report form. As I walked over to the crew room Lamont slapped my back.

"Well done, first operation in the bag. Let's get you a drink." He didn't mean any offense, but I found his words slightly condescending. It certainly wasn't my first operation, although it was the first time I'd flown a reconnaissance sortie over enemy territory. In the crew room I threw my kit over an armchair and Lamont produced a tin of fruit juice.

"There you go." he handed me the drink.

"Oh, thank you," I said with a hint of disappointment. When he said he would get me a drink I thought he was referring to something alcoholic.

I sat down and stared at the combat report. I was physically exhausted by the long flight, but my mind was racing. I quickly filled out the relevant boxes on the document and then pushed it to one side. Lamont had left the room so I pulled out my hip flask from the inside pocket of my uniform. The taste made me wince and I felt the world start to slow down.

"I'm sorry sir," I looked up to see Bertha standing in the doorway. I quickly tucked the hipflask down the side of the chair. "I'm afraid Flight Lieutenant Prowse is on the war path and wants to see you."

"Why?"

"It's the photographs you've brought back." I felt a rush of panic, had I pressed the wrong buttons or forgotten to flick the right switches? She must have read the expression on my face as she quickly added. "There's nothing wrong with them. They're very good, it's just the order they've been taken in. The instructions were to fly over Bergen first." My heart sank, I'd forgotten the negatives would be in the order I took them. I'd been betrayed by my own handy work. I swallowed hard, I had disobeyed a direct order, but if I got the photographs did it bloody matter? I thought for a moment.

"I'll go over and see him now." I looked down at the combat report on which I'd detailed all my actions. "Oh, would you mind getting me another blank form? I'm afraid I've made a hash of this one." I screwed up the paper and pushed it into my pocket.

"Certainly sir."

Prowse was in the darkroom where my film had just been developed and was hanging from the drying rack. He was holding one end of the roll and studying the negative image.

"What's the meaning of this?" He pointed to the film.

"I'm sorry sir, I'm not sure what's wrong." I looked at him blankly.

"Your orders were to fly to Bergen first and then Måløy. It appears you flew to Måløy first!"

"Oh … I'm sorry sir, I meant to tell you when I landed. When I arrived over Bergen the town was covered with patches of cloud, so I flew on to Måløy and then returned to Bergen afterwards when the sky was clear." I didn't like lying, but I didn't want to give Prowse the satisfaction of disciplining me. After all, I was risking my life and quite frankly I still didn't see what difference it made.

"You should have reported that the moment you landed!" he snarled.

"Yes sir. Won't happen again."

Outside, I lit a cigarette and looked up at the clouds. As much as I'd enjoyed the challenge of navigation and airmanship I was surprised that I'd found parts of the sortie pretty tedious. It was certainly different from the excitement and thrill that I had been used to on fighter operations.

"Here is the form you asked for sir," said Bertha when I walked back into the crew room. "Let's hope you don't make any mistakes on that one." She gave a wry smile.

# Chapter 10

## Complacency and distraction

Over the next few weeks, I carried out a number of similar sorties and by the end of the month I had a comprehensive knowledge of Southern Norway. Often the targets were small coastal ports. Lamont told me there was great concern over Norwegian fish oil being transported to Germany. I'd assumed it was to help with Nazi food production, but he corrected me.

"No, it's the glycerine they're after. It's a main component of high explosive."

Once I was given a roving commission to search for shipping. This was a more exciting sortie. I flew a low level course through a group of fjords, hoping to use the oblique camera but apart from an old sailing barge, I found nothing of interest.

I had no idea how lucky I had been, all these operations went ahead without any problems. I had no mechanical issues and the only enemy aircraft I came into contact with was a Focke-Wulf Condor, a long range maritime patrol aircraft, which passed several thousand feet below me one day.

With all this good fortune I began to grow bored and became complacent about safety. The boredom in turn manifested into restlessness. At the time I was unaware of how deeply I'd been affected by the events I'd experienced during the Battle of Britain. The constant strain of combat had shredded my nerves and six months on I was plagued by dark anxiety. At first I'd thought it was some form of heart complaint as I had a racing pulse and slight tremor in the hands. It came on in the evenings and I'd had some terrible nights lying awake in bed. I would lose all sense of proportion and find myself fixating on some peculiar issue which in the darkness appeared much larger than it was. Rarely did I consciously reflect on the incidents I'd witnessed over that summer, but those horrific images were buried deep within my memory.

I developed different ways of coping with the anxiety. One was to keep myself physically busy and the second was to drink. At first, I'd used alcohol to fortify my nerves, now it had subtly crept into my routine and I relied on it too much. On an operation a tot of whisky before taking off was a comfort, after landing it was a reward. In the mess pints of beer helped oil the wheels of conversation and encouraged the laughter. The real danger was when I was bored and unsettled. During periods of inactivity, when my mind was free to race away, a small drink would slow the world down. But these small drinks were often followed by larger ones.

The challenges I'd faced at Heston and when I'd arrived at Wick had kept my mind occupied. Now the routine of the unit was starting to drag and I unwittingly allowed myself to slip into a bad habit. I was also struggling with the social dynamic of the PR unit, it was quite different from a frontline squadron. In the air an effective fighter squadron had to work as a team, you hunted together and kept a vigilant eye out for each other. However, in a PR unit each pilot was completely on his own. He led the operation, he defended himself and until he was back on the ground, he was autonomous in the decision making. This kind of flying attracted a certain type of pilot, they were loners. This was reflected in their social habits, both Lamont and Kalman tended to keep themselves to themselves. As a result, I started to make new friends amongst the Coastal Command crews, as these boys were often up for a drinking session.

One evening, to celebrate a successful attack on a U-boat, one of the Hudson crews threw a raucous party in the mess. Due to thick layers of cloud and bad weather I had not flown any operations of my own for two days. I was bored stiff and the party was a welcome distraction, but I dramatically overindulged and was violently ill. The following day, as I lay shivering under the blankets and regretting every drop of whisky that had passed my lips, I reprimanded myself and vowed to change my ways.

When my hangover finally subsided and the weather cleared I was given the task of air testing another new Spitfire which had just been delivered. I took off and put the aircraft through its paces. After I was satisfied that the airframe and engine was all up together I dived down and headed back at low level over the Scottish countryside. As I crested the top of a hill I spotted a small castle that sat on the banks of a loch. I had noticed it before on other flights and was intrigued by the four square towers which rose above the main building. It looked like a romantic piece of architecture from some Scandinavian fairy tale. I turned towards it keeping low and following the contours of the valley. I passed over the flagpole at about three hundred feet and skimmed over the loch.

I arrived back at Wick and was pouring myself a coffee in the crew room when the telephone rang in the outer office. Through the thin wall I could hear Lamont muttering in a very serious tone. A moment later he appeared at the door.

"We've got a bit of a problem, Jack," he said as I added a lump of sugar into my mug.

"Oh, what's up?"

"I'm sorry, but it appears Sir Robert Hall has made a complaint."

"What about?"

"Low flying." Lamont twisted his lip. "I don't suppose you happened to buzz a castle this morning did you?" Not wanting to confess to the crime I shrugged my shoulders. Lamont frowned. "I'm afraid his butler noted down the tail number."

"Oh," I sighed, I was banged to rights. "Who is Robert Hall?" I asked.

"A big landowner in the area. He's also a member of parliament. I'm afraid the Station Commander want's you over at his office now."

Ten minutes later I found myself standing to attention in front of a large wooden desk, behind which sat the Station Commander. He was a big man in his forties with a set of thick black eyebrows that almost touched each other.

"Well, want to explain yourself sonny?" He leant one elbow on the desk and glared at me.

"I'm sorry sir, it's just I thought the castle was a good landmark to practise my low level photography on." The Station Commander shook his head at the feeble excuse.

"We have designated training areas for that kind of thing and you bloody know it!" He thumped the table. "You've put me in an awkward position. The last thing I need is an irate politician on my back."

"I'm sorry sir." He ignored my apology and scribbled something illegible down on a piece of paper.

"I'm putting you on a charge." My heart sank and my shoulders sagged. "Seeing as this is your first offence, if you behave yourself I'll consider dropping the case. But mess around again and I'll start docking your pay. Is that clear?" He looked up at me with a look that suggested I needed to leave his office as quickly as I could.

"Yes sir." I saluted smartly and turned away. I spent a good deal of that evening in a furious mood cursing Sir Robert and his miserable butler who got my number.

Despite the charge against me flying continued as normal. Most of the sorties were straight forward high altitude operations, which I found little challenge in carrying out. As long as the weather was clear my main concern was keeping myself entertained as I flew over the hundreds of miles of sea.

I needed a distraction, something I could focus my excess energy on. With this in mind I attempted an approach on Jenny, the attractive WAAF who worked in the interpretation room. There was a lack of females on the station and on forays into nearby areas we had found the local girls were as uncultivated as the moorland that surrounded the airfield. I started my campaign on Jenny by inventing excuses to visit the interpretation room and attempting to chat her up. I was careful to plan these sorties when Prowse wasn't around.

"I've come to check on the photographs I took yesterday," I said one morning. "I'm concerned the exposure may have been off." Jenny was standing over the table annotating some negatives. She'd taken off her tunic and was working in her shirt sleeves.

"I don't think there was any problem. They looked fine to me."

"Good, I was very concerned," I stammered stupidly.

"We're just about to have a tea break, can I get you some?"

Through these visits I managed to learn a little about her. She'd been billeted in a crofter's cottage just outside the station with three other WAAFs. Her family had been great industrialists and her father was a politician with some minor role in the cabinet. In all our conversations there had been no mention of a husband or fiancé, although a pilot from one of the Coastal Command squadrons appeared to be very keen on her. After a week of information gathering I asked her out.

"I'm afraid I haven't got an afternoon off until next week," she explained. "And I have had another offer, so wherever you were planning to take me needs to be better than my first offer."

"So, who's my rival then?"

"I'm afraid that's strictly confidential."

"Where's he taking you?"

"Oh, I'm not telling you that, it'll spoil the fun. You'll have to take a chance and come up with something better than he does."

She gave that faint smile again and went back to work. I was determined to give her my best shot, but I didn't like my chances. Once again I was short on money and opportunities for quality entertainment around Wick were non-existent. I needed to be creative with the limited resources I had.

However, all thoughts of any romantic interludes were interrupted the following day when I was given a task which would push the limits of my navigation and the endurance of the Spitfire.

Prowse had called me to his office. He was studying a map that was pinned to the wall. As I entered he turned and glanced at me briefly.

"Your orders are," he stressed the word orders, "to photograph the town of Aalborg." Using a ruler, he pointed to the northeast tip of Denmark. "From there, you are to fly north to Norway and make a pass over the Solvik fjord, continue on for several miles and then strike a course home." I looked at the map and tried to calculate the distance. I estimated it was a round trip of a thousand miles, three to four hours flying time. Prowse handed me the orders, which gave no more information except a rubber stamp mark that read urgent priority.

"Get airborne as soon as you can." I set to work

planning the route. Once again Bertha provided me with the information I needed.

"I wonder why this place Aalborg is so important?" I thought out loud.

"Radar," she answered. "It's the most northern point of the German air defences."

The route I planned was quite simple but very long. A southeast bearing from Wick would get me to the Danish Coast in about an hour and a half and over the first target about ten minutes later. My navigation needed to be dead on. As a rule of thumb, being just a single degree off course would mean for every sixty miles I travelled I'd be a mile off track. I'd flown long legs before, but never this long. The rest of the course was straight forward, although even Bertha had no idea why they wanted photographs of the fjord. I had a suspicion they were searching for battleships, but this fjord didn't appear to be that big.

It was early afternoon, if I could be airborne before fifteen hundred I should be back well before sunset. I telephoned the hangar and instructed the maintenance crew to have the Spitfire ready for me as soon as they could. After a quick sandwich and cup of coffee I picked up my gear and headed out to the airfield.

The pale blue Spitfire was parked up on the edge of the apron. Around the cockpit was a cluster of men. One of them, a wireless mechanic, was perched awkwardly with his head stuck down by the seat and his legs sticking skywards.

"What's going on?" I asked another man who was unbuttoning one of the fuselage panels.

"The radio ain't working."

"What's wrong with it?"

"Not sure yet, it's not transmitting. We're checking the connections again, but it looks like we might need to change the set."

I sighed with frustration, Lamont was airborne in the other Spitfire so I had no choice but to wait for the radio to be fixed. I walked back to the crew room and dragged a chair outside. For an hour I sat fidgeting with my fingers and obsessively checking my watch. I'd mentally prepared myself for the operation and was desperate to get airborne.

I watched one of the Lockheed Hudsons taxi by and head out towards the airfield. I could see the pilot carry out his checks, then the twin radial engines powered up and the aircraft rumbled down the runway. It lifted up into the air and disappeared out towards the horizon. I thought about the crew on board, for the next six or seven hours they'd have nothing to look at except the vast grey sea.

The wireless mechanic came over to me.

"The radio is completely dead, I'm sorry I'm going to have to replace the set."

"How long is that going to take?" I tried hard to suppress my irritation.

"We've just sent King over for a new one. When he gets back it'll probably take me about half an hour to fit it." I looked at my watch it was nearly four o'clock, I needed to be airborne or I'd lose the light.

"Bugger it! Don't worry about the radio, I can manage without. I need to get going."

"Are you sure sir?"

"Yes, just put her back together as best you can and I'll

get on my way," I snapped impatiently.

In the end I was airborne at sixteen-o-four. I scribbled the time down on my knee pad and turned the Spitfire out towards Denmark. Having no working radio wasn't a great concern on a reconnaissance operation. I might have needed it for a navigational fix, but I could only do that on the way home. Transmitting anywhere near enemy territory could give my position away. Besides, I was on my own, there was simply no one else to talk to up there.

I climbed to twenty thousand feet and settled into my usual routine of checking the compass, the engine instruments and counting down the time. It was a pleasant afternoon, only a few wispy layers of cloud sat between me and the sea below.

Below I could just make out a small boat chugging north. It looked miniscule against the huge expanse of water. I wondered how on earth the Vikings managed to navigate the same stretch of sea in their longships.

I checked the time and my heading, then let my mind wander towards Jenny and how I could impress her. It was a pity I'd had to leave the Bentley at Heston, with a car I could have taken her out somewhere. I could have done with my greatcoat as well.

At seventeen-thirty-seven the oil pressure was still good, and the Danish coast came into view. I hit the coastline about three miles south of my waypoint. A quick calculation told me I had drifted three degrees off course. I congratulated myself on my navigation and corrected the bearing.

I ran straight in over Aalborg and made two long passes

with the camera mechanism whirring away. Then as planned, I turned north towards Norway. I found the Solvik fjord and before engaging the camera I flew some wide circuits to study the shape of the coastline and check I was in the right place. So much of the Norwegian coast looked the same from up high it was all too easy to get confused. When I was satisfied, I levelled off and made the two required passes. With the operation complete I headed home on a direct course which took me over the southwest corner of the country.

I was beginning to feel weary and my legs were becoming stiff, so one at a time I stretched them out as best I could. I was starting to struggle with these laborious operations. I knew they were incredibly important, but I wondered if my skills as a fighter pilot could have been used to better effect somewhere else. I reviewed my options - I could stick it out at Wick and hope for the best, but I was also finding the area very dull. As beautiful as the Scottish countryside was, we were miles away from any cities or even a decent sized town. I could apply to return to a fighter squadron, but after the effort they'd made training me I didn't think that would go down too well. Maybe I could request a posting to somewhere interesting overseas.

I was deep in thought when out of the corner of my eye I noticed a little orange spot streak past the canopy. It was like the glowing end of a discarded cigarette, travelling in a dead straight line. It could have easily been mistaken for a ray of sunlight flaring through the Perspex, but I knew exactly what it was, a round of tracer. Someone had crept up behind me and was shooting.

In an instant my instincts as a fighter pilot overcame me. I pulled the control column hard back and to the right, at the same time I pushed the throttle forward. The Spitfire shot upwards in a steep vertical climb. The force of the violent manoeuvre pushed me hard into the seat. I felt the control column snatch and the aircraft juddered. I continued to pull back until I was almost inverted and heading towards where the tracer had come from. As I looked down through the canopy the menacing grey shape of a Messerschmitt 109 flashed directly underneath me. It was a fleeting glimpse, but I caught sight of the mottled grey camouflage, the two large black crosses outlined in white and the pilot's face staring up at me.

I presumed he was fairly inexperienced. For three minutes I had been flying straight and level, blissfully unaware that anyone else was in that patch of Norwegian sky. He had the perfect opportunity to fly up behind and riddle me with bullets. I'd have been none the wiser, but he had evidently opened fire from too far away which gave me that slim chance to escape.

I knew that when caught in an ambush the best defence is to run towards the enemy. It sounds counterintuitive, but by doing this you have a chance of getting behind whoever is shooting at you and this is what I'd done by pulling up and turning back towards the Messerschmitt. If I'd tried to simply run away I'd have been an easy target for his second burst of fire.

The impulse to pull up had saved my life. I'd responded so quickly the pilot had obviously been taken by surprise, although I was not out of the woods yet. I assumed the 109 would now turn hard and try to get behind me again. That fighter pilot instinct urged me to do the same and for a brief moment I forgot I was unarmed. I found my fingers looking for the brass gun button that wasn't there. Singleton's words of advice came thundering into my mind 'Your best means of survival will be speed and navigation.' I rolled the Spitfire level dropped the nose slightly and then ran like hell.

I was careful not to lose too much altitude, in a dogfight maintaining height advantage was critical. The evasive manoeuvre had pointed me towards the southeast on a heading that would take me over the coast. This was the best direction to run as my pursuer would probably be less inclined to follow me out over the sea. My airspeed rose rapidly as I drew every ounce of power from the Merlin engine. Each one of my limbs was rigid with fear. My eyes were glued to the mirror above my head which gave a limited view over the rear of the aircraft and the white clouds beyond. I expected at any moment to see that angular profile of the Messerschmitt reappear and another burst of gun fire to rip me apart. However, nothing happened.

I continued towards the sea at a rapid pace. If I had thrown off my pursuer there may be other fighters around who were now looking for me. I crossed the coast and, thank God, had the forethought to look at my watch and note the bearing I was on.

I loosened my shoulder straps and twisted round to look behind me, all seemed clear. I climbed slowly back up to twenty thousand feet where I felt safe enough to turn and check the sky more thoroughly. I gave out a great sigh of relief, I was alone and safe.

Incidents like this play very slowly in memory. It could only have been a matter of seconds from seeing that orange tracer to pulling the manoeuvre over the top, but the whole action seemed to take hours and etched in my mind was the image of the pilot looking up at me from his cockpit.

Now I was about twenty miles out to sea with the sun behind me. According to my original route plan I should have been heading back over the sea towards Wick by now. However, I'd just flown about seventy miles in the wrong direction. I had a rough idea of where I was and made some notes on my knee pad. The quickest way home would be to take a direct course over the southwest tip of Norway. I didn't like that idea much, as that would take me near to where I'd been attacked and I had a notion they might still be looking for me. I decided to head south for another five minutes then head northwest. This was a much longer route and instead of enemy fighters I'd have two other issues to worry about, how much fuel was left and when it would get dark.

As I pushed on out over the sea I started to calm down. On the map I marked off my progress. I drew a circle around the area where the 109 had appeared, it would be useful to avoid that area in future. I'd been attacked about twenty-five miles north of Kristiansand. I knew that name, Lamont had told me there was a large airfield near to the town. It dawned on me that like an idiot, I'd flown straight into a wasp's nest - there was I, just a few minutes earlier, thinking how bored and unchallenged I was.

I made a note of the time again and calculated when I was likely to make landfall. If I was lucky I should see Wick at twenty-hundred, that would be on the edge of darkness. I was desperate to stick the throttle forward and get home as quickly as possible, but I had to be careful about how much fuel I burnt.

I held the course for an hour, it was becoming gloomy outside and I was starting to get nervous. The thin white needle of the fuel gauge said I had fifteen gallons left, barely enough to take me home. I throttled back and started to descend. I stared hard into the horizon searching for the coast. If my radio had been working I could have called up for a fix and been directed home. I cursed myself for being so cocksure and not waiting for the radio set to be replaced. I anxiously checked the map again, but dared not make any corrections, I had to trust my navigation.

A surge of adrenaline began to rise up inside me again and I felt my back prickle with sweat. If I didn't see the coast soon I would have to ditch the aircraft and hope for the best. The thought of ditching made me panic. Not only would I have to survive in the icy cold sea, I would also lose the photographs that I'd risked my life to take. I was angry with myself for being so complacent. If I was going to die on that operation it would be my own stupid fault.

Then, with just ten gallons reading on the gauge I saw the faint outline of some land ahead. My heart lifted, I had a chance of reaching home without getting wet. I was flying lower now and could see angry swells rolling up on the water beneath me, almost as if the sea had realised she wouldn't be claiming me tonight.

In the fading light I struggled to make out the features of the coastline. It was unfamiliar to me and for a moment I worried that it wasn't Britain, but I reasoned that it had to be. I had under ten minutes of fuel left and no idea where to put the aircraft down. Just then, off my starboard wing I spotted a lighthouse. By sheer luck I recognised it as the Rattray Head Lighthouse, slightly to the southeast of Fraserburgh. It wasn't illuminated, few lighthouses were during wartime, but the last rays of sunlight were catching the distinctive shape of the tower. I was lucky, another minute and it wouldn't have been visible.

I knew a direct course northeast would get me to Wick, but that would take me over the sea again for at least five minutes. It was now dusk and finding any airfield was going to be very difficult. I reckoned I knew the airfield at Wick well enough to land in the dark, but I wasn't sure I had enough fuel to get me there. My options were limited, I could crash land where I was and potentially loose the photographs or try and make it home. I bit my lip and turned towards Wick.

It was getting hard to read the instruments in the cockpit. I could just make out the bearing on the compass, but there wasn't much point in trying to read the fuel gauge, if I was to run out of fuel there was nothing I could do about it now.

My heart was racing again, I was fully expecting the engine to die at any moment. I opened the canopy and the wind whipped around my neck. I leant out slightly, but it was hard to see anything as my goggles had misted up with the moisture from my brow. I flew on and on until I recognised the familiar contours of the land ahead and started to throttle back. I flicked the switch to bring down the flaps and lowered the undercarriage. The three tiny green lights glowed on the panel to show my wheels were down.

In front of me I could make out the shape of the hangars but couldn't see the runway. I just had to judge my position from memory and feel my way down. As I descended everything around me became darker until at about a hundred feet everything outside the aircraft became pitch black. For an agonising moment I was devoid of sight and then smack, a jolt through my spine told me I was down. It was a heavy landing, but I had her under control. Halfway along the runway there was a great bump and I felt the aircraft slew sideways. I squeezed the brake lever gently and came to a stop. Quickly, I shut the engine down and turned off the switches. I threw open the door and peered out into the darkness. I was completely disoriented and couldn't make out any features. As I climbed out onto the wing I saw the dim lights of a vehicle approaching, it was a crash tender.

"You okay there?" shouted the driver.

"Yes, I think so."

As my eyes adjusted to the darkness I started to make out where I was and what had happened. I'd run off the tarmac runway and ended up on the far side of the airfield.

"We heard you coming in and thought you were going to flip over." The driver climbed out of his cab. He looked up at the aircraft and then at the two long ruts my wheels had cut into the soft earth.

Presently my mud covered Spitfire was towed up to the hangars. I found Lamont waiting with an anxious expression on his face.

"I thought we'd lost you." He offered a cigarette. I felt my body start to shake and a chill overcame me. For two hours my nerves had been taut. Now as I relaxed and the adrenaline eased off I felt the true strain of what I'd just been through. I reached into my pocket and found my hipflask.

"Bloody hell!" came a shout from the mechanic who was removing the film canister. "Have you seen this sir?" He was speaking to Prowse who had driven over and stood watching them from the side. The mechanic had a screwdriver in his hand and was prodding a large hole in the metal panel that sat just behind the cockpit. It was a jagged puncture about an inch in diameter.

"What on earth did that?" asked Prowse with a bemused expression.

"A bullet or judging by the size I'd say a canon shell," I said nonchalantly.

"You were shot at?" Prowse seemed genuinely shocked by what he'd seen.

"Yes, and by the looks of things the bugger got me." I remembered the jolt I'd felt when I pulled up vertically. That must have been the shell hitting me.

Prowse gave me a long sideways glance as if he didn't believe me, but the evidence of the action was there in front of him.

"Blimey, it goes all the way through," said the mechanic who had found the exit hole on the other side of the aircraft. Prowse studied the hole with interest and then turned back to look at me.

"My God that was only inches away from the back of your seat," he said with amazement. "It could have killed you!" It was obvious that Prowse had never seen an aircraft return with damage from combat, I was surprised. I reached out and gently touched the sharp edge of the shell hole. I'd learnt not to get excited about such things. In the end, if a bullet missed you by an inch or a mile it still missed you.

Back in the crew room Prowse grilled me on what had happened. Briefly he lost his usual sharp officious manner and seemed genuinely fascinated by what I had to tell. He made copious notes about the 109 and what I could remember about the incident.

I always found debriefings taxing. Having to relive and explain what happened on an operation was mentally exhausting. I also found the process had a tendency to set a lot of doubt in my mind - was I remembering the details correctly? Had I taken the right actions? Did they believe what I was saying?

By the end of the interview Prowse's caustic mannerisms suddenly returned and he curtly turned me out of his office. Lamont, who was waiting in the crew room, offered me a lift back to the mess.

"I think the drinks are on me tonight old boy, we should just make last orders." He started the engine of his little Austin Seven. A stiff drink would have been very welcome, but the thrill of the operation had woken a new energy in me and there was something I needed to do before I could unwind.

"Would you mind if we made a detour?" I asked.

"No problem, where to?"

We drove out through the main gates of the station and down a narrow lane which ran alongside the perimeter fence. Nestled in amongst the long grass and thistles was a small cottage.

"I won't be a moment." I jumped out of the car and walked up the gravel path. The black out curtains were drawn across the windows and only a few thin slivers of warm light suggested anyone was at home. I knocked loudly on the low wooden door. After a moment there was a scraping of bolts and with a clunk it opened cautiously.

"Hello?" said a young woman from within. She had a thin pale face and wore a woollen dressing gown.

"Good evening," I said trying to sound formal, but also unthreatening. "Can you pass a message to Section Officer Winfrith?" The woman appeared to be surprised by the request and she looked at me with an air of suspicion. I wasn't surprised, after the long flight my uniform was creased and my hair was dishevelled. "It's most urgent," I added.

"She's upstairs, shall I get her?" The woman went to step back from the door.

"No," I said firmly. "Please can you ask her to be outside the station gates at one o'clock tomorrow afternoon."

# Chapter 11

## The stolen lunch

I pulled up at the station gates on a Norton motorcycle. It was an old machine with a dent in the fuel tank and a sidecar attached to the frame. Jenny folded her arms and gave me a quizzical look.

"Where on earth did you get that contraption?" she asked. It had been a bold move of mine, but I fancied Jenny had a good sense of humour and would be game for an adventure.

"If you must know I've hired it from one of the cooks." I pointed towards the sidecar. "Now hop in because I've got to return it before six."

"You must be joking!"

"No I'm not, I've been to a lot of trouble to organise our afternoon so get in."

She hitched up her uniform skirt and climbed into the sidecar as gracefully as she could.

"Where are we going?"

"It's a surprise."

"Don't go too fast, you'll mess up my hair."

I let the clutch out and we lurched forward. The road

ahead was dead straight with drystone walls neatly lining the fields that flanked each side. The area was mainly farmland and sparsely populated. The early afternoon sun was warming the earth and encouraging the crops to grow. Every so often we'd pass a cottage and attract a stern look from a crofter's wife or a friendly wave from a child. Conversation was impossible with the wind rushing past and the put-put of the engine, so I couldn't tell if Jenny was enjoying the experience or hating every moment. The Norton was a relatively slow machine, but I found it fun to be riding along and clunking through the gears.

Presently we turned down a narrow lane which rose slightly and then dropped down towards the sea. We passed some farm buildings where a group of men were loading a cart. An old nag startled at the sound of the motorcycle and I veered to avoid her. One of the farm hands dropped the fork he was holding and grabbed her reins. I carried on down the lane until we came to a dead end, beyond which a short gravel path ran to a beach. I pulled up and stopped the engine.

"You're bloody mad!" Jenny exclaimed.

"I know." I swung myself off the saddle. "Here, pass me the basket from under your feet." She reached into the side car and with a struggle pulled out a small wicker basket.

"What's inside?" she asked.

"Madame, I offer you a Royal Air Force picnic. If you'd like to follow me we will find a table with the best sea view." I offered her my hand and she climbed out.

The little path twisted and turned between some rocks and then opened out into a narrow sandy beach which curved around to form a bay. At the far end sat the wreck of the boat that I'd seen so many times from the air. It was an old steam launch with a rotten deck and rusty funnel. The cold clear water lapped gently on the beach and a soft breeze playfully shook the tall grass on the dunes behind.

"It's gorgeous." Jenny took in the view. "So do you take all your girls here?" She asked sarcastically.

"No, you're the first. I only know about this place because we use that wreck down there as a landmark." I pointed towards the launch.

"I was only teasing you. So, where's this picnic, I'm hungry."

We found a flat area of dry sand and I produced a grey service issue blanket from the basket. With an over exaggerated flick I placed it on the ground as if I was a snobbish waiter in a French bistro. Jenny laughed and I gestured for her to sit down. I rummaged deeper into the basket and pulled out some parcels of food wrapped in brown paper.

"For the first course we have a slice of pork pie, for the main ham sandwiches and lastly for dessert we have scones and a little bit of jam." It was hardly a luxury hamper from Fortnum's, but as far as wartime rationing went it was a decent spread. It had cost me a pretty penny too. I'd arranged with the cook, who had also hired out his motorcycle, to supply the food. I'm not sure where he had sourced it from, but I had a suspicion most of it had been stolen from the Officers' Mess.

Jenny surveyed the fare that I laid out before her.

"I'm genuinely impressed, you are very creative. I was

142

expecting you'd just take me to the pictures."

"I gave it a lot of thought and decided you would appreciate something different. Oh, I almost forgot, to accompany the meal we have a bottle of cider." I pulled out a green glass bottle and two enamel mugs.

All of a sudden the peaceful atmosphere of the bay was interrupted by one of the Coastal Command Whitley's climbing out from the airfield behind us.

"I hope that isn't my rival spying on us," I said as the aircraft turned and headed out to sea.

"I doubt it, he flies Hudsons." Jenny took one of the mugs and I unscrewed the cap of the cider.

"So, is he still a rival?" I asked tentatively.

"Oh yes, but I'd say you've got the edge at the moment. By the way he's picking me up at five o'clock."

"And where is he taking you?" My face fell.

"He's taking me out to dinner in his car." She was an incredible flirt, revelling in the attention it brought her. Her act was simple. She made herself approachable and yet at the same time unobtainable. As infuriating as she was, I have to say I was enjoying the sport.

"Now you're going to have to work hard, compared to you he's got one more engine on his aeroplane and one more wheel on his motor."

"Yes, but my aeroplane is a lot faster," I said with a sneer.

"Let's forget him for now." She picked up one of the sandwiches and began to unwrap it. As we dined on the stolen food I learnt a little more about her. As the daughter of a wealthy peer her upbringing had been quite different from my lower middle class life in Oxfordshire.

"I'd enjoyed my school days and the time I spent abroad, but my father is very traditional and was beginning to arrange a staggeringly dull future for me. I was all ready to be released into high society when, thank God, the war broke out," she told me. "You see I'm a bit of a tomboy and couldn't bear the thought of marriage, children and endless dinner parties talking politics. I volunteered immediately, much to father's dismay." She turned towards me and studied my face. "How about you? You know you're a bit of an enigma. You arrived one day out of the blue and I don't think I know anything about you."

"I'm afraid I'm very boring," I took a sip of the cider. "I was an apprentice engineer before the war and then I joined up."

"What about that?" She reached out and coquettishly ran her forefinger across my medal ribbon.

"Just lucky, that's all." I muttered. Jenny withdrew her hand and her expression changed. "I'm sorry, the damn thing makes me feel awkward," I explained. I picked up a porkpie and bit into it. "Come on eat up, this lot cost me a fortune," I said with a mouth full of pastry crust.

Jenny looked over towards the bay and her eye was caught by a sailing boat that had appeared off the head land. It was a slender looking craft with a black hull and a deep orange sail that billowed in the wind. "That's a fishing lugger." She pointed across the bay. "Do you sail?"

"No, never sailed before, although my father had a rowing skiff we'd take out on the Thames."

"You should try it, you'd be good at it. You know a sail

works exactly in the same way that an aeroplane's wing does."

"You seem to know a lot about it."

"We would go to Devon every year where my grandfather had several boats. My brothers and my cousins would go out for hours. We'd catch all kinds of fish."

I watched the little boat cutting gracefully through the water.

"Yes, I think I'd like sailing," I said thoughtfully.

Sitting on the rough blanket we ate the food and drank the cider as if we were attending Henley regatta. Beyond the horizon the sea that had seemed so treacherous to me the day before stretched out calm and tranquil. We walked off our lunch along the sandy beach, kicking pieces of driftwood and trying to skim any stones we found. For a few precious hours we forgot about the rigid rules of service life.

"What's it like flying over Norway?" she asked. "I'm always fascinated by the photographs we have to study. All those mountains and lakes, I'd love to go there one day."

"Lord knows what it's like on the ground, from the air it all seems very old and ancient. I suppose it's the mountains, even the Nazis can't bulldoze them or cut them down like you can with a forest. It must have looked the same for hundreds of generations and I imagine it'll stay the same for years to come." We had returned to the blanket and I poured out the last dregs of the cider.

"Do you enjoy the operations?"

"Sometimes," I took a sip from the mug. "For the most part they're pretty mundane. Every now and then something interesting happens, but in all honesty I'm starting to get bored."

"Oh," she said with surprise.

"I'm afraid I'm a bit of a restless soul. I was thinking about putting in for a transfer."

"Where would you go?"

"Not sure, somewhere hot hopefully."

Jenny leant forward and picked at a half eaten scone. Suddenly, a peculiar emotion was triggered deep within me. It was all too comfortable, I felt unguarded and vulnerable, as if there was a danger of letting her get too close to me. I looked at my watch. "I'd better be getting you back," I said abruptly. "You can't be late for your second date."

"I wouldn't worry, I have a feeling I'm going to get a terrible migraine and take to my bed."

She packed away the basket and I folded the blanket. As we walked back up to the motorcycle she took my arm. We arrived back at her cottage in good time and I saw her to the door.

"Thank you, it's been a lovely afternoon," she kissed my cheek and disappeared inside. I looked up and saw that a pair of eyes had been watching us from behind a net curtain. No doubt we would be a hot topic for the gossip mongers.

I rode back to the station in a dream-like state. It had been such a serene afternoon I was finding it hard to focus. In my reverie I drifted over the centre of the road and as I rounded a corner I was shocked to find myself travelling towards a dark green MG sports car. I swerved towards the verge and we narrowly missed each other. The driver leant furiously on his horn. He was an officer, just like me. I caught a glimpse of his serge blue uniform and set of pilot's wings. I recognised his face from the mess and suddenly realised that it was Jenny's second suitor on his way to pick her up. Hopefully her migraine had not suddenly cured itself. Good luck, I thought to myself as I watched the car over my shoulder.

I returned the motorcycle to the cook and handed over three pound notes to him. The picnic had been an expensive exercise and I'd had to take a loan from Lamont to finance it.

As I walked into the mess, a clerk handed me a message from Prowse, it said I was to report to him as soon as I returned. The pleasant sunny spring afternoon was suddenly far behind me.

I entered Prowse's office fully expecting a dressing down for some misdemeanour I'd innocently committed, however he hardly noticed me when I knocked. He was sitting behind his desk engrossed in a thick ream of papers.

"Take a seat," he said without looking up. I pulled out a wooden chair and sat down. Almost a full minute passed before he shuffled the papers together and spoke. "You've got orders to return to Solvik." He reached over for a cup which sat on a plain white saucer.

"Oh, when?"

"As soon as possible." He took a sip from the cup and passed over the orders. "I take it you don't have any worries about returning after what happened yesterday?" I was surprised by his comment and the flicker of concern that he showed. It seemed the canon shell I received through the fuselage had affected him more than me.

"No worries at all," I said firmly. "It would be best if I'm airborne just before first light. I'd prefer that to trying to come back in the dark again."

"Very well." He pulled over his black telephone and picked up the receiver. "I'll make sure the aircraft is ready."

The following morning I watched the dawn breaking over the North Sea from ten thousand feet. There was a bank of thick white cloud below me, which was predicted to clear before I reached the target. This time I planned to fly a similar route in the opposite direction.

Strangely, the orders were very specific and unlike any that I had received for a sortie before. They required me to photograph the mouth of the Solvik fjord at low level. We had no further requests so Prowse and I had picked out some decoy targets as well. Once over the coastline I intended to drop down low and hopefully keep under the enemy radar.

Everything went according to plan. I flew a crooked route over a steel factory and small town and then turned south towards the fjord. After being caught unawares on the last operation I now took every precaution I could. I kept low and would turn sharply at regular intervals. I scanned the sky for any fighters, but no one seemed interested in me today.

This was more like it, I thought to myself as I skimmed over the Norwegian landscape. I found the fjord and made two long passes at three hundred feet. Then I headed out to sea still keeping low. When I judged I was far enough away from any danger I climbed back up above the clouds.

I turned lazily on to the heading home, bearing two-three-zero and trimmed the aircraft off. I was just starting to think about what I could have for breakfast, when I heard the pitch of the engine alter. It was a very small change, but enough to concern me. I looked over the instruments, the oil pressure was good and so was the radiator temperature, but the RPM indicator showed a drop in power and the needle was fidgeting back and forth. I throttled forward and then back hoping the issue would clear, but instead of running up smoothly the engine spluttered. I was at fifteen thousand feet with two hundred and fifty miles of sea still to cross. It wasn't a good situation, although I had to count my blessings, fifteen thousand feet gave me a fighting chance. I was still cruising at a decent speed, but didn't have the power to climb any higher and the misfire seemed to be getting worse.

I had no choice but to keep on course and hope to God that the engine would hold out. I felt a cold clutch of anxiety start to grip me. In some ways situations like these were worse than facing the enemy, then you would have a rush of adrenaline that pulled you through. You had no opportunity to feel anxious in the middle of a dog fight.

To keep my airspeed up I was having to descend at a shallow angle, at present I was losing two hundred feet per minute. If I continued at that rate I'd be at two thousand feet within an hour and have to bail out. I checked my navigation and figured that I needed to maintain the course for an hour and thirty minutes to be in range of a rescue boat. It was going to be a very close call.

I tweaked the throttle again on the off chance that the

misfire would clear, it didn't work. The minutes on my watch ticked by slowly, but I knew that every mile I covered made my chances of survival greater. At two hundred miles out, I set the transmitter to gain a fix and then spoke into the radio, thank God it was working this time.

"This is Flycatcher calling, can anyone hear me?"

I waited nervously, but there was no response. Out of the corner of my eye I noticed I was now at eleven thousand feet. I tried again.

"Flycatcher, this is Flycatcher calling, can anyone hear me….can anyone hear me?" I could hear the desperation in my own voice. Then to my relief I heard a crackle in my headphones.

"Flycatcher, this is Chestnut control. We're receiving you."

"Chestnut, can you give me a fix?"

"Flycatcher, this is Chestnut, please wait." Another thirty seconds of agonising silence.

"Flycatcher, we have you one hundred and ninety miles east of Peterhead. What is your intention?"

"Chestnut, I have an engine problem and I'm losing altitude. I need to get back to the nearest airfield."

"Understood Flycatcher, please wait." Another minute passed by. "Flycatcher, your nearest airfield is Dyce. Please turn onto bearing two-five-zero for two hundred and forty miles." I wasted no time in taking the bearing, then I unfolded the map and found the airfield at Dyce. It was just outside Aberdeen.

"Flycatcher, do you require any further assistance?" The operator had a friendly voice and it was a great comfort to hear another human.

"Hello, Chestnut. Not at the moment, but if I can keep in touch with you until I have the coast in sight."

"Understood," there was a pleasant chuckle in the background. "I'm glad we can be of help."

I'd had to drop the nose down further to keep the speed up and was now at ten thousand feet. There was still nothing to do but fly a dead straight course. Then at eight thousand feet the engine perked up a little. The misfire was still there, but I'd gained a little power and could level off. It occurred to me the change in air pressure would have helped. The higher you rise, the thinner the air gets and a piston engine will lose power. As I was coming down the air was getting thicker and I was gaining power.

"Flycatcher, this is Chestnut. How are you proceeding?"

"I'm doing good thank you. Now at six thousand feet but levelled out."

"Understood, by the way you are now one hundred miles from the airfield."

I pushed on and on, my mood lightening with every mile covered. At twenty miles out the coast appeared.

"Chestnut, I'm at four thousand feet and can see the coast."

"Flycatcher, keep on the same bearing and the airfield will be four miles inland. I've let them know you're on your way."

"Thank you Chestnut."

"Good luck Flycatcher, Godspeed."

That last comment seemed to echo around my head and I wondered that if I attended church a little more often I'd have a better chance of survival. Then again dear old Gilroy was a devoted Catholic and it didn't seem to make any difference for him.

The coastline passed underneath me and as Chestnut had predicted the airfield appeared a few miles inland. By now the engine was very sick, which made landing difficult. Fortunately though, it was a large grass strip with plenty of space. I touched down as best I could and taxied the aircraft off the airfield. I was glad to be down again, for the second time in three days my flying abilities had been tested to the extreme.

I found a telephone in one of the hangars and managed to get a call through to Prowse. He duly dispatched an Avro Anson transport aircraft with two of our erks. I lay down beside the Spitfire and waited for them. They arrived about an hour and a half later. In a matter of minutes, they diagnosed the issue as a fault on the ignition system and estimated it would take several hours to remedy. Leaving them to it I flew back to Wick as a passenger in the Anson with the all important film canisters between my legs.

I was tired and ravenous by the time I reached Wick and after reporting to Prowse I made my way over to the mess. As I came up to the hangars I heard an unfamiliar engine noise echoing around the buildings. I looked over and saw a strange aircraft approaching the airfield. It had a large high wing and two radial engines which sat above its wide fuselage. It was quite unlike any aircraft I'd ever seen before. I stopped dead in my tracks, concerned that it was an enemy bomber starting an attack run. As I was considering whether or not to take cover I caught a glimpse of a red, white and blue RAF roundel painted on its side. I was grateful that I'd not thrown myself on the ground and made an idiot of myself. The aircraft touched down on the runway and disappeared out of my view.

I had missed breakfast, but the cook who had hired his motorcycle to me, provided a large plate of toast and jam. As much as I was hungry my nerves were still jittery and I had trouble digesting the meal. Halfway through I felt a pain shoot across my abdomen. I finished what I could, then stood up and tried to walk off the discomfort. I found a narrow bookcase in the corner of the room with a small selection of dust covered novels. I pulled one down and looked at the cover. It was bound in blue with a picture of a sailing boat embossed in gold. I thought back to the lugger Jenny and I had seen tacking out to sea. I took the novel into a quiet nook in the lounge and started to thumb through the pages. However, I struggled to make it past the first chapter. As always I was finding it hard to relax after a sortie and my mind bounced erratically from one thought to another. At some point fatigue overcame me and I fell into a deep sleep.

At dinner I met up with Lamont.

"I gather you had another exciting op then." he said sitting down beside me.

"Yes, bloody hairy."

"I've sent Kalman down to bring your Spit back."

The mess steward brought over a platter of cold meat.

"Have you given any more thought to joining the rugby team?" He helped himself to a bread roll and two slices of beef.

"Sorry, just not my game." I shook my head.

"Pity, we're still two men short." I didn't want to let him down, but I considered that if I was going to be put out of action it would be better by a German bullet than an overweight prop forward.

"Is that a new crew?" I nodded towards a table where two pilots and a navigator were sitting on their own. Lamont turned and squinted over his shoulder.

"Yes they came in earlier today."

"So, they were in that aircraft that landed earlier. What on earth is it?" I asked.

"A flying boat of all things, one of the new American Catalinas." Lamont gave his beef a liberal covering of salt. "I say flying boat, it's actually an amphibian, so it's capable of flying from land or water. They are mainly used for maritime patrols. I presume it's something to do with the Coastal Command chaps."

"I thought it looked strange."

"I gather those Catalinas have an incredible endurance. They can stay airborne for something like twenty hours."

"Christ, I get bored after two, I don't think I could hack a flight that long."

# Chapter 12

## An operation of huge importance

The following afternoon I sat alone in the crew room. Lamont was up on a sortie and Kalman had been given the day off. Apart from a test flight that was scheduled for later in the day, I had little to do so took the opportunity to make some progress with the book I'd found in the mess. This time I made good ground and had reached the fourth chapter when my concentration was broken by a screech of brakes on the road outside. I looked up to see a large black staff car with the Station Commander's pennant proudly sticking up from the radiator. The driver, a dark haired man, leapt out and charged up to the hut.

"Is Pilot Officer Sommers here?" he panted.

"Yes, that's me."

"Urgent message from the Station Commander, I'm to take you over to him."

"Why?"

"Dunno, sir. I was just ordered to bring you over."

"Now?"

"Yes, sir."

What on earth was all this about, I wondered. Maybe

that damn low flying charge was being escalated. Begrudgingly, I picked up my cap and followed him out into the car. He drove quickly across the front of the big hangars to the watch office, a two storey brick building which sat on the edge of the airfield.

By the looks of it something strange was going on. A different Anson transport aircraft had arrived and was parked alongside. There was also another staff car and an officer, with a revolver on his white webbing belt, waiting for us.

"You're to go straight in." The officer instructed me as I stepped out. He opened the door and I followed him in. We walked quickly down the corridor with our footsteps echoing loudly off the rough plaster walls. The building had recently been finished, there was a strong smell of fresh paint and sawdust. He stopped outside an unmarked green door and knocked.

"Come," snapped a voice. The officer opened the door and with a flick of his head encouraged me to enter. It was dark inside, heavy blackout curtains had been pulled over the two windows although it was only the middle of the afternoon. A single lightbulb shone down on a wooden table, around which sat three men. It looked as though we were interrupting an intense poker game, but there were no cards or green baize cloth. The Station Commander sat with his fists clenched in front of him. To his left sat a pilot, I recognised him as one of the crew from the Catalina that I'd seen in the mess the night before. Facing him was another man, he sat slightly in the shadow and I couldn't see his face, although I could make out the rank and insignia of a naval uniform. I heard the door close behind me.

"Take a seat," said the Station Commander. I gingerly pulled out a folding wooden chair and sat down. The room became hazy for a moment as I tried to comprehend the situation in front of me. Why had I been summoned? What was this secrecy all about?

"This is Flying Officer Murphy from Coastal Command and this is Commander Collings of Naval Intelligence." The shadowy figure leant forward into the light. I saw he was a man of about fifty with light auburn hair and a short beard. His eyes were alert and his rugged face looked as if it had weathered several heavy storms.

"Good morning," he said sternly.

"Sommers I'm asking you to volunteer for an operation of huge importance," announced the Station Commander in a formal tone. "I cannot give you any information about what's involved. If you agree you will not be allowed to talk to anyone apart from the people in this room or Murphy's crew until the operation has been completed. Afterwards you will not be allowed to discuss the operation.

"It's also important for you to understand that due to the nature of the operation it's highly likely that your efforts will also be unrewarded," added Collings. "In other words, there'll be no medals or mentions in dispatches."

"When you say volunteer, do I have a choice sir?" I asked the Station Commander.

"Put it this way, if you say no I'll be very disappointed." I thought about the low flying charge which was still sitting on his desk.

"I'd better say yes then, sir."

"Good," He relaxed his hands. "An operation has been planned for this evening. It involves the rescue of a person from enemy territory. Murphy and his Catalina crew have been tasked with the operation. We have however hit a snag. I'll let Murphy fill you in on the details." Murphy shuffled his chair towards the table and looked at me. He spoke slowly with the hint of an Irish accent.

"We had an issue with our port engine on the way over. The spark plugs were changed this morning, my co-pilot, Singer, supervised the work. He was checking the cowlings had been fitted back correctly when the ladder he was using gave way. He fell from a fair height and has broken his ankle."

"Obviously he can't fly and we need to replace him." The Station Commander cut across the table and pointed a firm finger towards me. "That's where you come in. You'll fly as co-pilot."

"But ... I've never flown a Catalina," I stammered with confusion.

"You don't need to fly the damn thing, just sit in as co-pilot," the Station Commander dismissed my concern with a wave of his right hand. "Besides, you have experience on twin engine aircraft don't you."

"A few hours on Oxfords, but that's all."

"You weren't the first choice." Murphy quickly interjected with a sneer. "It's a short trip and I can handle the Cat on my own, I don't need a co-pilot."

"That is out of the question." Collings spoke firmly from the shadows. "The success of the operation is crucial and I insist that you fly with a co-pilot. We can't take a chance of anything happening to you."

Murphy slouched back in his chair with a sullen frown. I wasn't keen on his attitude towards me, but I did share his sentiment.

"Are you sure I'm the right man for the job?" I pleaded.

"There is another Catalina crew at Castle Archdale in Northern Ireland, but they're fog bound and it's not likely to lift until this evening. That doesn't leave enough time to fly over here and prepare for the operation," explained the Station Commander.

"Wouldn't one of the Hudson pilots be more suitable?"

"Yes they would!" he barked impatiently "but you have a unique experience." I noticed his eyebrow lifted slightly.

"Oh, what's that?" I asked stupidly.

"I gather your knowledge of the area is the best we've got. You've been photographing the exact location where the pickup is due to take place - the Solvik Fjord." Now I knew why they'd been so interested in the fjord. "You can fly a twin engine aircraft, your navigation is good and your knowledge is excellent. It seems like you're the perfect man for the job." The Station Commander picked up his cap and gloves from the table and rose from his chair. "The details of the operation are highly secret, so I'll leave Commander Collings to brief you. In the meantime, I'll make sure you have everything you need for the operation. Good morning gentlemen and good luck." He turned smartly and left the room. I sat staring at his empty chair and wondering how on earth I'd managed to get myself into this predicament. Immediately the door closed, Collings turned to the officer with the revolver.

"Ask the rest of Flight Lieutenant Murphy's crew to come in." A moment later another three men were ushered into the room.

"Please sit down gentlemen." Collings had a rigid and determined intonation in his voice, but he didn't bark orders like other senior officers, he had a far more subtle manner in dealing with people. With a lot of screeching and scraping each man drew out a chair and sat down. Murphy, who until then had been lounging back in his chair, suddenly sat forward and addressed his crew.

"Right, listen in. As you know Singer has broken his ankle. However, tonight's job is still on." He cast me a frosty glance. "This is Pilot Officer Sommers who will now be flying as co-pilot for this operation." I felt three pairs of eyes stare squarely at me, I gave an awkward smile in return. Then one by one Murphy introduced his crew. The first was a tall man with a square jaw and thick black moustache, he was Flight Sergeant Merrill the Flight engineer. The second was Smith, the wireless operator, a young man who I judged was still a teenager. He had thin lips, sharp eyes and ears that appeared to be too large for his head. Lastly was the navigator, Pilot Officer Harvey. He had an athletic build and mop of unkempt blonde hair. On first impression they looked like a strange assortment of characters, but it was clear to see that they were all loyal to Murphy.

"As you've probably guessed our job tonight is a rescue operation from enemy territory," he spoke sternly, looking at each of his men in turn. "There's a lot to take in, so pin back your lugholes." He sat back and let Collings take up the briefing.

"You will only be told what you need to know. This is a very dangerous operation. If anything goes wrong and you are captured it's likely that you'll be interrogated. Therefore, the less you know the better." I swallowed hard. Collings glanced at a sheet of paper in front of him and continued.

"The aim of the operation is to pick up and bring back a single person from Norway. Tonight, you will fly to the Solvik Fjord and there are very specific instructions for when you land. At exactly zero-one-hundred a short flare path will be lit between two pontoons on the fjord. Your approach will be from the south and you will land your aircraft on the water, approximately fifty yards to the left of the flares. You will then taxi up towards the village at the end of the fjord and turn around. You will wait until a rowing boat approaches. With a torch the person in the boat will signal the codeword 'dogrose' in morse code. You will acknowledge with the codeword 'bookmark'. Once alongside, the person will climb into the aircraft via the rear access. There will only be one person and he will be carrying a canvas bag. As soon as he's inside and safe, you will take off and fly straight back here to Wick. Once you arrive back here, the person will immediately be transferred to me."

There was a tense silence as each of us processed what the orders meant. It sounded like a very straightforward set of instructions, but in essence we were being told to land in enemy territory and pick up a spy. Judging by the grim expressions around the table, each one of us understood the magnitude of the operation.

Collings leant forward, lit a cigarette and then offered the packet around. The atmosphere relaxed slightly.

"The fjord has been chosen because there is very little German presence in the area. There is a garrison of troops about twenty miles away and some of the waterways are patrolled by fast gun boats, but there are only a few of them. However, as you well know, you only need a single bullet hole in the wrong place and the operation will end in disaster." Collings looked towards Murphy. "I suggest you keep the engines running when you land and then position your crew in the best defensive positions."

"Yes, Harvey will take up the front gun turret, I want Merrill at his station in case of engine issues and Smithy will man the Browning's in the rear." I was just wondering what I was to do when Murphy turned towards me. "That leaves you to get the agent on board. As soon as we land you go to the rear of the aircraft and wait for his signal. I hope your morse code is up to scratch."

"Yes, it's good." I said sharply.

"All of you are to be issued with revolvers. I take it you know how to use them?" asked Collings. "Sommers, in addition you'll be given a sub-machine gun just in case the passenger has been compromised and you find yourself dealing with problems."

I nodded as nonchalantly as I could, but I was becoming quite overwhelmed with the situation. It was starting to sound like the plot of a gangster movie rather than a rescue operation.

"Your arrival needs to be spot on time. Once you're on the water and in position, wait for no more than ten minutes. If you see no signal then you are to take off and return as quickly as possible."

Collings then produced a canvas map case from under the table and took out a large scale chart. "This is the suggested route." He picked up a short wooden ruler and used it to demonstrate the course over the chart. "From Wick you fly directly east southeast for four hundred miles. This takes you slap bang into the middle of the Skagerrak straits. There is a full moon this evening which will help with navigation. Then you turn northeast and follow the coastline up for one hundred miles, here you turn due north and you'll come in straight towards the Solvik Fjord. God willing, you'll see the flare path from there."

"And the route home?" asked Harvey in a clipped accent.

"The same in reverse," Collings answered.

"I don't want to come out the way we went in," objected Murphy. "If we get spotted arriving they might try and catch us on the way out."

"The alternative would be a direct course west over land," suggested Harvey.

"I'd prefer that," said Murphy. Collings looked over.

"Sommers you know the area. What would you do?" All the faces in the room turned towards me, I pulled nervously at my chin and carefully considered my answer.

"The route in makes sense, but I'd make sure we keep as low as we could and as far from the coastline. I think it could be very risky to take a direct course back. There's a lot of high ground and mountains to the west. What altitude will we be at?"

"We'll be high enough," Murphy replied flippantly.

"He's got a point Skipper," Harvey interjected. "We'd have to climb quite high to get out that way." Murphy pulled the chart towards him and studied the figures which marked off the height of the terrain. I looked over towards Harvey.

"There's another danger to the west and that's the fighter station at Kristiansand. I bumped into a 109 there several days ago. I'd opt for heading south and straight back out to sea."

"What range does a 109 have?" asked Harvey.

"I imagine it's similar to a normal Spitfire, about three to four hundred miles," I answered vaguely. Harvey stabbed his finger at Kristiansand and stretched his thumb as if he was using his hand as a map divider.

"So as soon as we are three miles from this coastline we're in danger of interception," he was clearly surprised.

"Oh yes. That's why it's imperative that this operation is carried out at night," said Collings. Murphy looked up from the chart.

"We can't afford to be anywhere near the coast in daylight." He shifted in his seat and looked at his crew. "We will fly out to the southwest over the sea and keep below two thousand feet. And let's hope they won't be able to find us in the dark." He appeared to have taken some of the advice on board, albeit reluctantly.

"These should be familiar to you Sommers." Collings reached into the map case again and laid out a set of prints on the table. They were the photographs of the fjord that I had taken over the last week. One was a top view which had been annotated with pen marks.

"This is the area where the flare path will be lit." Collings used his wooden ruler again. "And the passenger should approach you from this bank."

"How high is this land around the fjord?" Murphy asked.

"The heights are marked on the chart, but thanks to Sommers we also have these oblique views which give you a good idea of the terrain." Collings pushed over the other prints.

"I'd say your best landing approach is in directly from the south," I suggested.

"Yeah," Murphy grunted.

"What's up here?" asked Harvey referring to a collection of buildings.

"It's a small village, a few small cottages and some boat sheds," said Collings.

I looked at the photograph remembering the red topped roofs and whitewashed walls of the pretty looking houses.

"What altitude were these taken at?" Murphy asked.

"About four hundred feet," I replied.

For almost half an hour we poured over the maps and charts until a plan was agreed on. Then it was down to Harvey to work out what time we needed to be airborne. From his own bag he took out a set of instruments and set to work calculating the speeds and distances. We watched as he measured the course and then scribbled down some figures with a thick pencil.

"It's five hundred and fifty miles, depending on the headwind that should take us about four hours and twenty-four minutes." It surprised me how long he estimated the flight would be, but then the Catalina was much slower than a Spitfire. I was used to covering that distance in half the time.

"The flare path will be lit at zero-one-hundred. You'll need to be overhead just before," said Collings.

"In which case we need to be airborne at twenty-thirty-five," Harvey looked to Murphy who confirmed the suggestion with a nod. "If we allow ten minutes to get our passenger on board we should be able to make it back home before sunrise." I looked at my watch, it was approaching five thirty. In three hours' time we would be on our way.

"I suggest you start preparing yourselves," said Collings.

In a large room alongside our equipment had been placed on a set of trestle tables. Neatly laid out were four Enfield 2 revolvers and a Thompson sub machine gun. There were boxes of ammunition for each weapon and webbing belts with holsters for the revolvers.

"You'll need to sign for each of these," said Collings and he passed around a clipboard.

I looked down at the sub machine gun with curiosity. I'd handle many different rifles and firearms, but the Tommy gun was a novelty to me. The butt stock and grip were made of a dark wood. The thin barrel and breach were machined from steel. On the table were three empty magazines and two long cardboard boxes with '.45 Colt Auto' printed on the top. I picked up the weapon and was surprised by its weight.

"Have you used one before?" asked Collings.

"No, I can't say that I have."

"Okay, it's fairly simple." He took the weapon from me.

166

"It takes twenty rounds in the mag." He slotted an empty magazine into the bottom of the breach with a firm click. He then reached for the short cocking handle on the right and drew it back. "There's two catches here." He turned the weapon over. "This one is the safety and this one is the selective fire." He took the safety catch off and squeezed the trigger, there was a snap and the bolt flew forward. "If you select full auto and fire you'll burn through a magazine in two to three seconds. I recommend you keep it on single shot." He handed it back to me. "Remember, it's a short range weapon, very effective in close quarters, but pretty useless over two hundred feet. Never try to fire it from the hip." I raised the stock up and jammed it into my shoulder. My eyes ran down the barrel and fixed on the sight at the end. I took aim at a clock on the far wall and felt a boyish thrill as I imagined firing a burst of bullets into an advancing enemy. Then I lowered the barrel and wondered whether I would really have the guts to pull the trigger. Merrill, the Flight Engineer, was standing alongside me. With his hand he snapped the chamber of the revolver shut and tucked it into his holster.

"Let's hope we don't have to use 'em," he said dryly. Murphy handed me the clipboard with the documents to sign. He gave a disdainful look at the Thompson in my hand.

"Don't go letting that thing off in my aircraft."

"I wasn't intending to."

"Yeah, well make sure you keep the safety catch on." He snatched the clipboard back and walked away.

"Don't worry about the Skipper, he's always wary of new

faces." whispered Harvey as we filed back into the other room. "We are a tight crew and it takes a lot to win his trust." He opened the door for me. "The trouble is you Spitfire pilots do have a reputation of being prima donnas."

Harvey had a point, as pilots we certainly had had more than our fair share of the limelight. However, I didn't feel like defending myself. I was already nervous about the operation and I didn't want to waste energy trying to win the trust of a man who seemed to be downright rude.

Back at the table we double checked our figures for the sortie. Merrill had calculated the fuel consumption of the engines. In terms of the Catalina's endurance this would be an easy trip. The fuel tanks could carry ten times more than my Spitfire and that was enough to do the whole operation twice over.

We were brought a hot meal of ham and eggs. I ate what I could, but again my nerves were getting the better of me and I was beginning to feel nauseous. There was now nothing else to do but wait. Smithy produced a pack of cards and offered a game of gin rummy, but no one was interested in playing. For three quarters of an hour, we stewed in an anxious smoky atmosphere. There were odd snatches of muttered conversation. I sat silently, feeling isolated and longing for my hipflask that I'd left in the crew room.

The tension was broken by a rap on the door and a message that our transport had arrived. We stood up and were beginning to gather our flying gear and weapons when Collings came back into the room and slammed down a bottle of malt whisky.

"In Scotland it's customary to have a quick tot before you depart." I looked at the amber liquid with delight. We each quickly found an enamel mug and Collings poured out the whiskey. I have to say I was disappointed at the size of the measure, but grateful for his gift. Then as if he was attending some old Celtic ritual he held his own mug up high and recited an old Scottish poem.

"So fill to me the parting glass and gather as the evening falls and gently rise and softly call goodnight and joy be to you all."

He took a large sip and swallowed hard. "Good luck gentleman." I raised my own mug up and savoured the taste. Smithy, who was standing alongside me, gave a wince as he downed his.

"It's an acquired taste," joked Harvey.

One by one we finished our drinks and left the empty mugs on the table. Outside a Fordson lorry was waiting for us.

# Chapter 13

## Take off at dusk

It was a short journey across the airfield. We all sat silently in the back of the lorry. Harvey had his eyes closed as if he was in deep meditation, Smithy stared out of the small round window, Merrill fidgeted with his flying helmet and Murphy sat forward with his finger and thumb pinching the bridge of his nose.

The driver pulled up and stopped. Smithy, who was nearest, turned the handle and opened the back door. We all squinted as the harsh rays of the setting sun shone directly into our faces. One at a time we climbed out and there in front of us, silhouetted against the vivid sky, was the big Catalina. Its large rudder fin stood up high like the sail of a yacht, above the hull shaped fuselage ran the long thick wing. The heavy propellors rested motionless on the front of two powerful Pratt and Whitney Twin Wasp engines. On the rear quarter of the fuselage, protruding like a pair of bulbous eyes, were the two clear Perspex observation blisters, the tops of which sparkled in the dying light.

With my leather jacket tucked under one arm and the sub machine gun and ammunition under the other, I

followed Smithy and Murphy across the concrete path. A
gentle breeze carried the sharp odour of high octane fuel
from the engines. We walked towards the rear of the aircraft
where an aluminium ladder leant against the open blister.
Smithy dropped his kit bag and scampered up the ladder
into the fuselage. Once inside he reached down and Murphy
handed up both kit bags. It was a well rehearsed movement
carried out without any conversation. Murphy climbed in
and I stepped to the foot of the ladder.

"Give me the gun and your gear," said Smithy peering
down at me. I reached up and gave him the jacket, then as
he took the machine gun one of the magazines slipped from
my arm. It clattered onto the concrete scattering several
rounds of ammunition underneath the fuselage. I quickly
bent down to pick up the magazine, but Harvey had already
got there and Merrill was chasing after the bullets which
were rolling around.

"What the hell was that!" I looked up and saw Murphy's
face glaring at me from the blister.

"Just one of the magazines, that's all."

"Well, hurry up and get in." I cursed my clumsiness, I
hadn't even got into the aircraft and things were going
wrong. I gathered myself together and climbed up the
ladder.

Inside, the fuselage was more spacious than it appeared
from the outside. A series of aluminium bulkheads
separated the aircraft into different compartments. The
rearmost, where the observation blisters were, was the
widest. Either side, two Browning machine guns were
mounted. Both of the weapons were glistening in oil and

171

hanging from the breaches were long links of ammunition. It would be Smithy's job to man these if we came under attack.

"You'll need this when we land." Smithy opened a metal box that was attached to the bulkhead and showed me the Aldis signal lamp inside. "It plugs in beneath the window and there's a spare bulb in the box." He pointed over towards an electrical connector.

I stooped low and climbed through a small rectangular door into the next compartment where four canvas bunk beds were fixed to the side of the fuselage. In the following compartment the roof line was higher, here I could stand without hitting my head, a novelty for most of the aircraft I'd flown in. To my surprise there was a two-ring gas hob on top of two metal lockers. Above, almost suspended in the air, was a seat, in front of which were a series of instruments and controls. This would be where Merrill would monitor the engines and switch the fuel supply between the different tanks. Now I had to climb through an even smaller door. Smithy came up from behind. He reached through and took the machine gun from me.

"I'll stow this down here with my stuff," he pointed to his own kit bag which was tucked under a desk. This was the radio and navigation compartment. On either side were small desks with metal chairs that swivelled and pivoted on an elaborate frame system. I stepped through and smashed the top of my head on the bulkhead. Fortunately, Smithy was looking down and didn't see. I winced and gritted my teeth.

Another small door led into the cockpit. To get into the

co-pilot seat I had to twist through the aperture and squeeze myself upwards. You had to be nimble to climb into a Spitfire, but it took a lot more pushing and pulling to climb into an aircraft like this. Murphy was already sitting down on the left hand side. He watched me as I sagged into my seat with a sigh.

"Are you okay?" he asked.

"Yes," I muttered.

He leant over and opened the small window to his left. Merrill was outside talking to one of the erks. Murphy shouted over to him and they proceeded through a list of checks. I heard some banging in the compartment behind and Harvey's head appeared through the door below our elbows.

"All good skipper, fifteen minutes before we need to be airborne."

I fiddled with the shoulder straps and tightened the harness. Then I stretched out my legs and adjusted the seat so the rudder bar sat evenly at my feet. Compared to the little Oxford from Heston the Catalina's cockpit was a lot sturdier and more comfortable. Laid out in front of me was a black panel with two sets of duplicated instruments and two large semicircular control yokes.

Collings had followed us across with the Station Commander and I could see them watching us from the edge of the apron. I remembered Singleton seeing me off from Heston. My God, that seemed like a decade ago and yet it could have only been weeks. I pushed back my jacket sleeve and looked at the watch he'd given me. I wondered what he would make of this peculiar operation.

I'd been given Singer's flying helmet to use as my own had different microphone connections. I was never keen on sharing another man's helmet as you tended to sweat in them and after a while they developed an odour. Inside this one Singer's name was written in large letters and a brown tidemark of Brylcream ran round the edge. Reluctantly, I pulled it over my head and took hold of the headset cable. Murphy reached over and showed me the intercom socket on the right hand side that I needed to plug into.

"When we start our take off run I need you to follow through on the throttle controls." He pointed up to the roof of the cockpit where two long levers hung down. Then he put his hand across to demonstrate. "I'll ease them forward until we get to about sixty knots, then I need to put both my hands on the yoke. You need to take over the throttles until we're airborne. Then, when I shout - pull these propeller pitch levers back." I rehearsed the movement and he appeared satisfied.

With a click he turned on the master battery switch and I heard a buzz in my headset as the electrical circuit came alive. He set the throttles and mixture controls, selected the fuel tanks and opened the engine cowl gills. He looked out of the window and shouted to Merrill again.

"Starting number one!" Merrill gave a thumbs up in response. Murphy turned the big magneto switch by his right knee and engaged the starter. There was a whining sound above my head as the starboard engine turned over on its battery and then with a great roar it started. I felt the aircraft begin to rock as the power built up. Merrill gave a nod and Murphy started the port engine. The instruments on the panel in front of me were alive now, the little white needles flickering as the temperatures and pressures rose. Merrill waited to check all was safe and then ran to the back of the aircraft. A moment later his head appeared below my elbow.

"They both look good skipper. A little white smoke on the port, but that cleared pretty quickly."

"Okay, get to your station now." Merrill disappeared back into the fuselage. Murphy waited for him to climb up into his chair and then spoke over the intercom.

"Everybody check in please." There followed a series of replies.

"Navigator here sir."

"Flight Engineer loud and clear Skipper."

"Wireless operator Skipper."

Murphy prompted me with a look.

"Co Pilot here Skipper."

"Okay everyone, make sure you keep the chatter down. Nav what time have you got?"

"Twenty-twenty-six, Skipper."

Murphy released the brakes and we started to roll forward. With a loud burst of throttle from the port engine he turned the Catalina around and started to taxi towards the runway.

Over towards the edge of the airfield I could just see the roof of Jenny's cottage. As I watched a thin line of smoke curled up from the chimney I conjured up the memory of our afternoon at the beach. I looked back to the instrument panel and focused my attention on the task ahead.

Murphy turned the aircraft to face down the centre line

of the runway. Flying off into a darkening sky was an unusual experience for me. I'd taken off in the dark plenty of times, but that was before sunrise when the day would get brighter and occasionally I'd had to land in the dark when timings had caught me out. However, this would be the first time I'd flown an entire operation at night. I was apprehensive, but Murphy's crew were used to such operations and the Catalina was well equipped for flying in the dark.

"You remember what to do?" Murphy shouted over the rumble of the engines.

"Yes, I remember."

He put his right hand up to the throttles and pushed them forward. The pitch of the engines rose as we started to move forwards. As we accelerated I could feel the aircraft wallow from side to side on its large wheels. The powerful engines were well balanced and Murphy didn't have to apply much rudder to keep her straight. I held my hand up ready. At sixty knots Murphy let go of the levers and I took control of the throttles. He pulled the yoke back firmly and I felt the nose wheel rise from the ground, a second later the main wheels lifted.

"Now!" he shouted and I pulled the two short levers that changed the pitch of the propellers. We were now on a steady climb and he toggled another switch to bring the undercarriage up. There was a high pitched whine as the motors retracted the wheels and then a series of thumps as they locked into place. I took my hands away from the throttles.

"Okay, well done," said Murphy over the intercom. His

voice was deadpan and I struggled to work out if the remark was genuine or sarcastic. Harvey's head poked through into the cockpit again.

"I make that airborne at twenty-thirty-four, skipper." He handed Murphy a scrap of paper. "Bearing zero-nine-eight for three hours twelve minutes."

"Bearing zero-nine-eight," Murphy repeated the instruction to show he'd understood Harvey's request. Then with a gentle movement on the yoke he dropped the port wing and banked the Catalina onto the course.

At two thousand feet Murphy levelled off. High above us a layer of cloud was thickening and below the last stubborn rays of the setting sun reflected off the wave tops. The sea was calm, but in the fading light the black water looked more treacherous than I'd ever seen it. We had a long flight ahead of us and with little to do but stare out into the night sky, I was beginning to feel anxious. Murphy, however, seemed to be in his element. Now we were airborne and on our way there was a sea change in his demeanour. He stretched out his legs and relaxed in his seat. When he was satisfied that all was good he spoke into the intercom.

"How are those engines looking Stu?" He asked Merrill.

"Not bad skipper, the smoke cleared on number two. Oil pressure is good."

"Okay, give me plenty of warning when you want to switch the fuel tanks over."

"Will do skipper."

"Navigator are you happy?"

"Yes, we're on track," answered Harvey.

"Sparks, how are the radios?"

"All good Skipper, valves are warm," came Smithy's reply.

"Are you okay to test the Brownings? I think we're far enough out now."

"Understood skipper, will do." There was a crackle and click as Smithy disconnected his headset and left his station. A minute later there was another click as he reached the waist guns and plugged back into the intercom.

"Skipper I'm on the port side gun. Can I go ahead and test it?"

"Yes, go ahead, just don't shoot the bloody tail plane off."

Even over the dull roar of the engines I could hear a thud thud thud echo through the fuselage as Smithy test fired the Browning machine gun. Then a moment later he fired the starboard side gun. It was reassuring to know we had some heavy duty firepower on board, but as with the Tommy gun, I hoped we wouldn't need to use them.

We flew on into the night with Murphy staring intensely at the instruments in front of him. Every so often he would make small adjustments on the yoke or toggle one of the switches. I sat beside him twiddling my thumbs. I could only wait now.

# Chapter 14

## Enemy coast ahead

We were halfway across the North Sea. As the clouds closed in above us the world outside the cockpit morphed into a dark blue nothingness. For a time it was impossible to distinguish what was sky and what was sea. To fly safely Murphy had to rely completely on instruments, I had been trained to do this as well but had never had cause to do so on an operation. I looked at the dials in front of me which were illuminated by a small pin light and fidgeted nervously. I never enjoyed placing my faith in another pilot's abilities.

"Cocoa?" Smithy had stuck his head through into the cockpit and was holding an enamel mug. Murphy looked over towards me.

"Hold her steady while I take a swig." I was surprised by his request and his confidence in me. I placed my hands on the yoke and took control.

"You got her?"

"I have control."

Murphy had been so precious about his aircraft I felt as if I was putting my arms around his wife and taking her for a slow dance. He watched me carefully over the rim of his mug as I held the aircraft on course.

"You want a cup?" he asked.

"Yeah, if there's one going," I replied nonchalantly.

"How do you take it?" asked Smithy.

"Strong, plenty of sugar."

When Murphy finished his drink he handed the mug to Smithy and took back control of the aircraft. Having a hot drink while flying was another new experience for me and I found it strangely relaxing. Coastal Command aircraft like the Catalina and the big four engine Sunderlands had been designed to undertake long maritime patrols and were equipped with kettles, stoves and even a toilet. Often they'd be airborne for twelve hours at a time, shadowing shipping convoys or searching for U-boats, so anything that made the operations more comfortable had been gladly welcomed. For this type of work the tight-knit crews had to have immense patience, they were a strange blend of seafarer and aviator. It was a completely different type of flying from the fast and furious operations of a fighter pilot.

As we flew on the clouds thinned out and the sky became lighter. Then as we reached the edge of the weather front the sky opened out above us. It was like the curtain opening on a stage set, one by one the stars appeared and the moon in its first quarter cast a white shimmer over the wave tops.

Harvey appeared between us again.

"One minute until change of course, skipper."

"Okay, thanks," said Murphy as he took another scrap of paper from him. Then pushing the mask to his face, he spoke into the intercom. "Smithy, make sure everything is tidy back there and get ready to man the waist guns when we've made the next turn."

"Will do skipper," Smithy replied.

I watched the minute pass by on my watch.

"Bearing zero-four-seven, skipper," Harvey's voice crackled over the intercom.

"Turning onto bearing zero-four-seven," Murphy repeated. With that he banked the port wing and turned towards the north. We were now close to Norway and flying parallel to the country's southern coastline. There was little danger that the enemy would appear, but there was every chance that some radar station or ship had detected our presence and we were now being watched.

"On this course for forty-eight minutes," Harvey's voice came calmly over the intercom. I noticed Murphy had tensed his shoulders and was sitting upright.

"Smithy, man the port gun and keep your eyes peeled. You see anything, you let me know right away." From the waist gun position Smithy acknowledge the order. Murphy pushed forward and we descended to a thousand feet.

"What's the fuel situation?" he asked Merrill.

"We've got plenty to get us there, over four hundred gallons before we need to switch over."

"Are you dead sure?" Murphy asked curtly. "I don't want to be screwing around with fuel tanks when we're on the water."

"Dead sure," Merrill barked back confidently. Evidently Murphy's mood had changed once more and as we neared the objective the atmosphere over the intercom was becoming tense. I strained my eyes to see if I could make out the coastline, but the horizon was still black and undefinable. Behind the cockpit Harvey moved the light on his plotting table, briefly it shone through a gap in the bulkhead and struck my cheeks. As I looked ahead I saw my face reflected in the glass windscreen. For a moment I thought I was staring at my father, the stress and strain of the last year had aged me. My cheeks were thin and dark shadows hung under my eyes. Harvey moved the light again and my reflection disappeared.

With no visual way of gauging our progress we had to count the minutes down. Time dragged by until we had to change course. This meant we were now only thirty-seven miles from the fjord. Murphy banked the wing again and turned onto the bearing which would take us straight to our objective. I felt the aircraft descend gently as Murphy pushed forward on the yoke. Now he levelled off at six hundred feet. I would have preferred him to stay higher, there were plenty of hills that stood taller than the height we were flying and if we were off course there was a danger that we'd fly straight into one.

Harvey leant into the cockpit again.

"We're bang on schedule, skipper."

Murphy spoke into the intercom.

"Okay everyone, keep a look out for the flare path. It should be lit as soon as they hear us."

I sat up in my seat and scanned my eyes carefully across the horizon. The moonlight cast a soft silver hue over the landscape as if we were flying onto the canvas of a romantic oil painting. Even in the dark I could make out the familiar contours of the fjord and looking down I recognised a series of shapes below us.

"Those are the islands at the mouth of the fjord," I pointed forward.

"You sure?" barked Murphy.

"Pretty much so, they're the same shape."

"There!" Harvey suddenly exclaimed and pointed over Murphy's shoulder. Slightly to the port side of the nose a tiny orange dot appeared, then behind it a second and then a third until a line of five flares stretched out across the water. Murphy banked to give himself a better view.

"Yes, that's our path for sure." Murphy confirmed the sighting. "We're too far to the right hand side. I'll head back to the south and make the approach again."

He made a long sweeping turn which brought us back over the mouth of the fjord and then turned again to line up with the flare path on the starboard side of the aircraft.

"Right, this is it, Nav take your position up in the front turret." There was a scuffling under my feet and I saw Harvey squeezing through the metal frames to get to the front gun turret. Murphy reached over to flick a switch and at the far end of the wings the tip floats extended. He pulled the throttles back and the pitch of the engines lowered. In front the flare path spread out like a torchlit procession. The orange flames reflecting on the water gave the only visual indication of how high we were. At three hundred feet above the water Murphy eased the yoke back and the aircraft began to flare. We appeared to hang in the air for several seconds until a hammering thud shuddered the fuselage and a great spray of water ran up over the nose. The landing was far more violent than I had expected. The friction of the water against the fuselage was so great it felt that the fjord had grabbed hold of the aircraft and was pulling us down.

Murphy had landed exactly in line with the flare path, in the dark that was no mean feat. He kept the revs up on the engines until we had passed the last flare and then shouted to me.

"Give me full left rudder." I followed his command and stepped hard on the rudder bar. At the same time he brought the starboard engine revs up and the aircraft started to turn quickly.

"Okay, that's enough," he said as we came to rest facing the direction that we had approached from. "Get back there and get that man on board."

I fumbled with the lap buckle and released my seat straps. I stood up and squeezed back down into the compartment behind. I nearly lost my balance as the aircraft was still settling on the water and rocking from side to side. I stopped by Smithy's position to pick up the Tommy gun. He had stowed the weapon under his table and I had to drop to my knees to retrieve it. As I stood up the trailing lead of my headset caught on the table leg and jarred my neck. It was impossible to move through this aircraft without smashing or straining some part of my body.

All the while the aluminium fuselage creaked and groaned as we bobbed up and down on the water. I reached the last compartment where Smithy was manning the port waist gun. He had one foot on the metal step and the handle of the big Browning machine gun resting at his fingertips. He was staring through the open blister, the moonlight behind casting him into silhouette. I scrambled into the opposite position and took the Aldis lamp from its box. Then I laid the Tommy gun down between my feet, took off my gloves and plugged in my headset and the lamp.

"I'm in position Skipper,"

"Okay, you see anything?"

I looked out of the blister, my eyes taking a little time to make sense of the darkness. We were about two hundred and fifty feet from a shoreline. I could clearly see the water directly in front of me, but beyond the rest of the fjord was pitch black and undefinable. A ridge of land seemed to rise up steeply behind to where a dense crop of pine trees stood, their distinctive branches and leaves standing out against the night sky.

"Nothing yet," I reported back.

I craned my head out of the blister. Behind us I could make out the edge of the bay where I presumed the little village was. Here and there the roof of a building jutted up and caught the light. I could hear nothing above the drone of the idling engines. I felt incredibly vulnerable with the sound reverberating around the landscape. I was sure every German soldier within fifty miles could hear the din, but at the same time there was a comfort knowing that the engines were running and we could escape quickly if needed.

I reached down for the Tommy gun, inserted a magazine and then cocked the weapon. It suddenly occurred to me that I couldn't remember which position the safety catch needed to be in and in the darkness I couldn't read the markings. There was every possibility I had it on fully automatic. I rested the barrel on the edge of the blister and hoped it wouldn't go off.

Those few seconds felt like an eternity. My limbs were tense and my hands had become clammy. Acrid fumes from the idling engines began to seep into the compartment and turn my stomach. I stared out across the water anxiously wishing for something to happen. Then I saw it, a tiny white light which flashed quickly.

"White light, two hundred feet off the starboard bow," I spurted excitedly over the intercom. I read the series of flashes. "He's given the code word, dogrose."

"Confirm the signal quickly," ordered Murphy.

I carefully placed the Tommy gun back down and picked up the Aldis lamp. As I aimed the beam towards the bank my mind went blank and for a terrible moment I thought I'd forgotten the code. However, I closed my eyes, took a breath and then almost subconsciously my fingers clicked out the reply word.

"Keep him covered as he gets near, if he's been compromised this still could be a trap." Murphy echoed Collings' warning. I dropped the lamp and picked the machine gun back up. I stared hard towards where the light had come from. The darkness played all manner of tricks on my eyes with phantom shapes quickly appearing and then disappearing.

"Can you see him yet?" Murphy was getting impatient.

"No," I snapped back. "Hold on, yes I can see something now."

The bow of a small rowing boat was cutting through the water about fifty feet away. Very slowly the shape became clearer, I could see the figure of a man and then the splash of an oar as he rowed towards us. He was making good progress with the long firm movements of a proficient boatman. By the time he was level with the wingtip float I could make out his features clearly. He was a well built man wearing a heavy white jumper and woollen hat. He slowed his stroke as he neared us and then turned his face up at me. I was expecting a hard weather beaten Nordic countenance, but instead he had sharp features and a dark complexion. I had kept the machine gun trained on him, but now I saw he had no weapon I lowered the barrel. He pulled in his oars and let the rowing boat glide towards the fuselage.

"Don't let him smack the aircraft and puncture the hull," warned Murphy. I was getting fed up with his nagging in my ear so I pulled off my headset and threw it down with the Aldis lamp.

"Hello," said the man with a broad smile. "Can you take this?" He threw the end of a rope painter up into the open window. I put down the machine gun and took up the slack in the line. He then handed up a large canvas backpack. I leant out and took it with my spare hand. Then surprisingly came one of the oars. I took it inside but couldn't understand why he wanted to keep it, I had a strange idea he might want us to take his rowing boat on board as well. However, he left the other oar behind and raised himself up onto the edge of the blister and vaulted into the fuselage. He took the oar from my hands and then leaning back out of the window used it to give the boat a strong shove and pushed it away from the aircraft. It was a sensible thought and something I'd overlooked, if the rowing boat caught on the aircraft it could cause all manner of problems. When he was satisfied that the boat was out of harm's way he pulled his arm back and launched the oar out of the window as if it was a spear.

"Pity, that was a nice boat," he said, looking out of the window. He turned and held out his hand "I'm Andersen," He spoke with a crystal clear English accent, although even in the dim light he didn't look very English.

"Hi, I'm Sommers."

"Skipper says he wants to get going sir," said Smithy who was still plugged into the intercom. I slammed the blister window shut and stooped down to pick up Andersen's backpack, but his large hand stopped me.

"I'd rather handle that myself, if you don't mind." I gave him a quizzical look. "It's rather precious," he explained as he grabbed the handle. To me it looked like an ordinary backpack and I wondered what on earth could be inside it, papers, photographs or maybe some top secret weapon.

"You'd better make yourself comfortable here." I took Andersen into the next compartment. He sat down on one of the bunks and I raced back up towards the cockpit. Harvey had come back in from the front turret and we had to struggle over each other as we met in the narrow passage.

"He's on board, we're good to go." I shouted jumping into the co-pilot's seat. Murphy's hand was already on the throttles. Without looking at me he pushed his hand forward, the engines above my head started to growl as they dragged the hull through the water. I settled into my seat and expelled a sigh of relief, glad that we were now on our way. Slowly the aircraft picked up speed and water started to spray over the nose. Then suddenly there was an almighty crack and we slewed violently to the left. As I'd not managed to fasten my straps I was thrown forward, my forehead smashing the instrument panel. Murphy pulled the throttles right back and the fuselage which had ridden up on the water sagged back down. I was thrown back into my seat dazed and confused.

"Shit! What was that?" shouted Murphy.

# Chapter 15

## Snagged

At first I thought we'd been hit by gunfire and expected more shots to follow, but nothing happened. I felt a trickle of liquid collect above my eye and then run down my face. I gently prodded my forehead and a sharp pain told me I had cut myself. It was painful, but apart from that I seemed to be in one piece. Murphy was peering out of the window, his right hand was still holding the engine throttles.

"What's happened?" I stuttered.

"We've struck something, but I can't see what it is." He turned and looked at me. "Are you all right?"

"Yeah, I think so."

"Get back there and see if you can work out what's happened." He took his hand from the throttles and gestured backwards with his thumb. Cautiously, I slipped out of my seat and down into the compartment behind. In the darkness I stepped on something soft and lumpy.

"Ow! That's my arm," yelled Harvey.

"What are you doing?"

"The bloody light's been smashed. Everything flew off the table. I'm trying to find my torch."

"Are we keeping the engines running?" Merrill called down from his position.

"Yes!" Murphy yelled from the cockpit. I stretched my leg over the bulk of Harvey's body and stumbled into the next compartment.

"Hello," I called out in the darkness.

"We're over here." Andersen called from up by the blisters. Harvey found his torch and turned it on. He shone it up through the fuselage, projecting my shadow on the bulkhead in front. Through the hazy combination of the torch beam and moonlight I could see Andersen crouching down and Smithy's body propped up against his knee.

"He's unconscious," explained Andersen. "He cracked his head on the gun barrel." Harvey swung his torch onto Smithy's face. He had no cut on his head like mine, instead there was a large red swelling on his left temple. His eyes were half closed and appeared unphased by the bright light. I stared down wondering what to do.

"What's his name?" asked Andersen as he shielded his eyes from the light.

"Smith," Harvey lowered the torch.

"No, his first name."

"Oh, Roy." Andersen crouched forward and spoke softly again.

"Roy, can you hear me?" Smithy's right eye flickered. "You've had a bang on the head, Roy." Andersen waved his open hand in front of the radio operator's face. "Can you see my fingers?" There was a slight nod of the head. Andersen looked up towards Harvey and me. "He's coming round. Help me get him on to one of the bunks in there."

191

Harvey handed me the torch then knelt forward and took the weight of Smithy's body while Andersen stood up. Carefully they shuffled the semi-conscious man along the aluminium footplates and then lifted him into one of the canvas bunks.

While they did this I climbed up to the gun position and looked out through the blister. After the bright torchlight it took my eyes a moment to adjust. I could make out a large dark shape protruding from under the port wingtip. I opened the window and shone the torch out. It wasn't a very strong beam, but it was bright enough to catch the stern of a sailing boat. Our wingtip was wedged on the deck and entangled in a mass of rigging and masts. I quickly turned the torch off as I didn't want to attract any attention, although the noise of the engines was probably doing that already. I hurried back to the front of the aircraft and shoved my head into the cockpit.

"Kill the engines," I panted.

"Why, what's happened?" demanded Murphy.

"We've collided with a boat. The float and wingtip are snagged up."

"No, we can't have," Murphy choked in disbelief. "Where did it come from?"

"It was probably moored in the middle of the fjord. You've got to kill the engines." I pleaded, but instead he grabbed hold of the throttles and pushed forward.

"Nonsense, we'll power on over the top," he shouted frantically. The engines whined as he increased the revs. I felt the aircraft start to move and for a moment I thought he might have cleared the obstruction, but we were not going forward, we were rotating around the tip.

"For God's sake stop, you're going to rip the wing off!" I shouted. With an angry swipe he pulled the throttles back.

"I can't risk stopping the engines, I'm worried they won't start again," he yelled.

"We're going to have to take that chance." He gave me a grave look and then begrudgingly flicked the magneto switches. The engines slowed and then sputtered to a stop. I stood looking at Murphy in the gloomy light. All was quiet except for the gentle slosh of water and creaking of the fuselage. It was a deceptively calm atmosphere which seemed to highlight our vulnerability. Harvey came up behind me.

"Smithy's been concussed."

"How?" asked Murphy, confused.

"Hit his head on one of the Brownings," Harvey explained.

I stood there fully expecting Murphy to start barking out orders, but he didn't, instead he just stared at us forlornly. Our situation was dire, we had an injured crew member, a trapped aircraft and a spy on board. If Murphy was incapable of reacting I had to seize the initiative.

"I'm going to get out on the wing and see if I can free us." I reached up and grabbed hold of the escape hatch handle which was set into the roof of the cockpit. I pulled it back with a violent movement. I climbed up on my seat and squeezed myself through the narrow opening. Above me the engines and propellers sat motionless. They were still hot and I could feel the heat radiating off the cowlings.

"Here take this." I looked down to see Harvey's delicate

hand passing his torch through the hatch. I took it from him and he started to climb through. I made my way backwards and by using a radio aerial to steady myself I struggled up onto the top of the wing. I tried to stand, but the smooth metal surface was soaking wet and slippery. Instead, I knelt down to steady myself and waited for Harvey to catch up. Only a few feet below the wing, the ice cold water of the fjord lapped against the fuselage. I reached out my hand and helped Harvey up. Carefully, the two of us crept along the wing. The gentle waves of the water and pressure of the wind made the aircraft sway. As we moved further out I worried that under our weight the wing might suddenly move and we'd slip off. However, the wing was set rigid and when we eventually reached the tip we found the float was tangled on the sailing boat's deck. With a click I switched on the torch and shone it over the chaos. It was difficult to make out what was boat and what was aircraft. It looked as though we'd hit her from the stern. The leading edge of the wing had cleared the transom at the rear, but then shattered a small mast, while the float had smashed through the wooden wheelhouse and hit the main mast. The large canvas sail had unfurled and was hanging limply over the deck. At the bow the anchor chain was pulling hard.

"Jesus, what a mess," exclaimed Harvey from behind me. "What's holding us up?"

"Not sure." I crept forward until I was directly over the boat. A rope halyard from the mast had caught on the wing. I handed the torch back to Harvey and then gripping the rope with both hands I tried to loosen it. However, it was so taut I could hardly wrap my fingers around it. I let go and cursed.

"We need a knife, have you got one?" I asked Harvey.

"Good God," he said ignoring my question. I followed his gaze to where the torch beam revealed a jagged gash in the wing. Protruding from the end and running down into the deck of the boat was a steel cable. The boat was evidently a fishing gaff and was equipped with a small crane for hauling up its nets. The steel cable we had snagged was part of the crane's rigging. It would take more than a knife to cut through that cable.

"Have we got any tools on board?" I asked Harvey.

"Nothing that will cut through that," he said with a shake of the head. "Do you think we could lever it off?"

"I doubt it. It's cut into the wing. Even this rope is too tight to pull off." I looked over towards the shoreline. We were a lot closer in than I thought. It occurred to me that in the time we had been waiting for Andersen to row to us we had slowly drifted sideways and our take off run had been about twenty degrees out. In the darkness Murphy had obviously not noticed and that was how we had collided with the boat. Judging by the way the steel cable was wrapped around the wing I assumed Murphy's attempt to power on through the obstruction had made the situation a lot worse.

"I'm going to climb down onto the deck and see if I can loosen the cable." I crawled to the very tip of the wing and gingerly swung my legs over. I lowered myself as far as I could and then let go. It was a fair drop on to the boat although my fall was softened by a pile of nets that were stacked to one side. I traced the line of the cable from the hole in the wing to the wreckage of the deck crane. One end fed back into a winch which sat under the float of the aircraft. The other was attached to the deck via a heavy steel plate and three dog clips.

"Can you free it?" Harvey asked from up on the wing.

"I don't know. Shine the torch down here." The beam fell on the three dog clips, they were red with rust and almost corroded into a single lump of metal. In the wreckage I saw a length of angle iron which had come apart from the crane arm. I reached down and with some difficulty managed to draw it out. Then I thrust it under the float of the aircraft and by using a lump of broken wood as a fulcrum attempted to lever the winch free. Using all my strength I pushed downwards, but all I managed to do was to tighten the wire and dent the float.

"What's it looking like?"

"Bloody terrible, we'd better get back and tell the Skipper what's happened." With some difficulty I clambered up onto the remains of the wheelhouse and crawled back onto the aircraft. Together we crept across the wing and climbed down through the hatch. Murphy was still sitting in his seat, both Andersen and Merrill had come forward and were leaning over through the bulkhead.

"We've hit a fishing boat. The float is resting on the deck and the wing has been snagged by a rope and a steel cable which has cut into the skin. We need tools to free off the rope and cable."

"What about the float?" asked Murphy.

"It's still intact. I tried levering it off, but the wire is

196

holding it fast." I wiped a bead of sweat from my forehead and made my wound smart.

"What about undoing the wire?" suggested Merrill.

"The only end I can get to is fixed with three rusty dog clips. If we had the right spanner we might be able to undo them. What tools have we got on board?"

"There's a crowbar and screwdriver set under the radios," shouted Harvey through the hatch above.

"I'm afraid that won't get us very far," I said glumly.

"Are you sure we can't just power through?" asked Merrill.

"No, we've already tried," grumbled Murphy.

"Besides, the cable will cut the wingtip and float off," I added.

"So, we're not getting out of here quickly," said Andersen thoughtfully. "I suggest we man the machine guns, just in case someone decides to take some pot shots at us."

"I'll do that," Merrill volunteered and shuffled back up to the blisters.

There was a fretful silence as we all contemplated our situation. I stared down at the floor desperately wracking my brain for a solution.

"Can you get me to the shore?" said Andersen suddenly. I looked up and squinted at him.

"Why?"

"There are plenty of boat sheds down by the village, no doubt there'll be something there we can cut ourselves free with."

I looked at Murphy, but he just shrugged his shoulders.

"There's an inflatable survival dinghy in the back, you could use that," suggested Harvey.

"Will that work?" I looked back at Andersen.

"I think so."

Harvey climbed down into the cockpit and followed us up to the rear compartment. He bent down under the bunk that Smithy was lying on and drew out a large canvas pack. We dragged it up to the starboard blister where Merrill was crouching by the waist guns.

"Help me throw this out of the window. We can't inflate it inside." Andersen grabbed one end and with a heave the two men launched the pack outside. As they did so Harvey pulled a cord triggering a gas bottle. There was a high pitch hiss and then a crackle as the canvas unfolded and the rubber dinghy inflated. It was circular in shape and much bigger than I had imagined it would be.

"Christ! It's massive," exclaimed Andersen.

"What did you expect? It's a survival dinghy not an admiral's barge," replied Harvey.

"Have you got any oars?"

"It comes with these." Harvey reached down and presented Andersen with two wooden paddles that were no bigger than a pair of tennis rackets.

"It's going to be a job to get that over to the shore," mused Andersen. "I'll need help." He looked across at Harvey who replied with an awkward grimace. I looked out across the water into the shadows of the shoreline and groaned.

"All right, I'll go with you," I volunteered reluctantly. Andersen smiled at me.

"Okay, probably best if you bring that gun of yours and did you say there was a crowbar somewhere?" He stepped back into the forward compartment and picked up his rucksack.

"Listen, if anything goes wrong and you think you're going to be captured, throw this over the side. It's weighted with rocks and won't float." He pushed the canvas bag into Harvey's hands. "Trust me, you don't want to get caught with it." Harvey held the bag awkwardly out in front of his chest and eyed it with concern. I took off my flying jacket and stuffed it under Smithy's bunk. A moment later I was scrambling through the window and following Andersen down into the bright yellow dinghy. I looked back up at Harvey and he handed me the machine gun, crowbar, paddles and a torch.

"Good luck," he whispered.

"Thanks, I think we're going to need it." I pointed over towards the shoreline. "Keep an eye out over there, I'll signal with the torch when we're coming back."

"What's the code?"

"Three short, three long."

With that I reached out and pushed off from the fuselage.

# Chapter 16

## Tool Thieves

Andersen knelt his big frame down on the left side of the dinghy, I took up position on the right.

"Keep it quiet and aim for that clump of trees." He pointed his paddle towards the bank.

The dinghy's circular shape was designed to keep it afloat in rough seas. As a result, it was an effort to keep it moving in a straight line, but the two of us found a rhythm with our paddles and slowly we started to make progress.

It was a surreal feeling sculling across the tranquil water in the moonlight. There was a crisp freshness in the air and a slight tang of salt lifting from the fjord. For a good five minutes we rowed as hard as we could. Every now and then a gust of wind would whip round and try to push us back. The work was heavy going and I was glad to rest my arms when we reached the shallows in front of the bank and the dinghy ran aground. Carefully we both climbed out. I felt cold water seep into my boots through the zip. Andersen pointed towards the trees.

"Pull the dinghy up there."

We each took hold of the thin rope which ran round the

outside of the rubber and lifted the dinghy. The shoreline was a chaotic mix of large rocks and pebbles, in the darkness it was difficult to move without tripping over or twisting an ankle. At the water's edge the trees had grown into the rough terrain and long twisted roots jutted out between the trunks. We laid the dinghy down under a large birch tree. I picked up the Tommy gun and torch.

"Don't turn that on," warned Andersen as he reached for the crowbar. I wondered if he meant the gun or the torch. He motioned me to crouch down.

"Stay here for a moment, I'm going to see what's up ahead." Keeping himself low he crept deeper into the woods.

I turned and looked out towards the fjord. Either the moon had become brighter or my eyes were adjusting to the dark for I could clearly see the Catalina stranded on the water. It looked very vulnerable. Surely we didn't have much time before somebody spotted it? I turned back and laid the barrel of the Tommy gun down on my leg. I cursed myself, in my haste I hadn't picked up the extra magazines. If we did get caught in a fire fight thirty rounds of ammunition would not be enough to fend off a persistent enemy.

Up ahead I sensed something moving. I assumed it was Andersen coming back and went to wave, but then a pang of fear came over me, what if it wasn't him? I stayed dead still watching the shadow as it came closer. It stopped about twenty feet in front of me.

"Hello?" whispered Andersen.

"Over here," I replied with relief. He moved slowly

towards me and I saw his grinning face in the dim light.

"Right, we're about a hundred yards from the main road to the village. I am pretty sure there's a boat yard about half a mile down the road."

"Do you know the village well? Are they friendly down there?" I asked in an anxious whisper. He was silent for a moment and then let out a sigh.

"Look you're going to have to trust me. The less you know about me and where I've been the better, just in case this all goes wrong. Let's say some people around here are more friendly than others." He shifted his feet and knelt down beside me. Using an open hand he gestured towards the left. "We'll go through the woods and keep parallel to the road. No one should be moving around at this time of night, but if we see or hear anything lie down and stay still." He sprung up on to his haunches. "Keep up with me, but not too close." He moved off silently through the trees. I slung the strap of the Tommy gun over my shoulder and started to follow him.

I watched him as he weaved carefully between the vegetation. For a big man he moved swiftly. Like a nervous animal, his head constantly twitched from side to side as he watched and listened for any dangers. He navigated the nocturnal Nordic landscape with ease and yet for me every dark shadow took the form of a man, every call of a bird sounded like a shout. At one point Andersen dropped back onto his knees, I stopped dead and did the same. He cocked his head to one side and peered towards a thick patch of ferns. I slowly slid the Tommy gun off my shoulder. Then a small deer burst out of the undergrowth and bolted away from us. The sudden movement startled me and my muscles tensed. I gave a sigh of relief and my warm breath formed a cloud which curled up in front of my face. Andersen waited for a moment and then moved off again.

Amongst the trees the air was cold and carried a sweet smell of pine sap. Underfoot the soft woodland floor was covered in leaves and needles making each footstep almost silent. On my left I could still see the water shimmering in the fjord and occasionally on my right I could see the surface of the road as it wound its way down to the village.

The going was tough and after ten minutes I was breathing heavily and struggling to keep up with Andersen, whose athletic ability was far beyond mine. Sweat was running down my back and my hands were shaking. Eventually we came to the edge of the woodland. Andersen stooped low and dropped down behind the trunk of an uprooted pine tree. I crept over and laid down beside him.

"That's the boat yard," he whispered.

In front of us the terrain dropped away and there was a large patch of open ground which narrowed as it reached the bank of the fjord. About two hundred yards away, set slightly back from the water was a large shed, outside of which I could see several boats in various states of repair. Alongside there was a ramshackle collection of buildings which I took to be cottages. They were neatly constructed with painted wooden walls and white windows. Two of them had smoke rising from their chimneys and the light of a fire dimly flickered in the downstairs of another. I looked back over the yard and in my mind the landscape all fell into place. Twice I'd flown over this very spot to photograph it,

I recognised the buildings and the yard. I thought of how those operations seemed so easy compared to the situation I was in now.

"Let's just wait for a moment and check it's all clear."

I adjusted my position and made myself comfortable. We were now a fair distance from the stranded aircraft and the small amount of safety it offered. As I looked out over the open patch of ground and the adrenaline wore off, a sense of fear began to build up inside me. Never before had I set foot on enemy territory and I certainly didn't feel prepared. As pilots we'd been given escape maps and compasses, but they were almost a token gesture and I for one never thought that I would need to use them. I was worried who was in those houses and whether they'd be hostile. I had no choice but to put all my faith in Andersen. I looked over at him. The darkness obscured his face, but I could make out his athletic figure crouching like a prowling mammal. Although we had only met an hour ago, had no formal introduction and knew very little about each other, our strange brief adventure had already bonded me closer to him than a decade of friendship.

Apart from the flickering light, nothing had moved before us. From deep in the woods came the call of a nocturnal bird and from a remote field the bleat of sheep. In the far distance I could make out the purr of a petrol engine.

"I can hear a car," I whispered urgently.

"No, that's a generator, probably down in the village," Andersen replied calmly. "I reckon it's clear." He pointed down towards the yard. "We'll move along that ditch." He raised himself up and crept forward. Once again I followed his lead and we edged our way out of the tree line. The ground was now mossy with tufts of damp grass which dragged against my trouser legs.

The perimeter of the boat yard was marked out by a low wooden fence. Using a post to steady his hand, Andersen vaulted over in a single bound. My attempt was less successful, the seat of my trouser snagged on the fence and I would have fallen to the ground had he not caught my arm and arrested my fall.

"Thanks," I whispered and we both knelt down beside a large wooden crate.

"There's probably a door around the other side. They don't tend to lock their buildings around here so hopefully it should be easy to get in. If not I'll try the crowbar."

I looked up at the boat shed, it was made of corrugated iron and like the other buildings it had a rugged neatness. Cautiously we began to creep around the yard. We passed by two upturned sailing boats and had to climb over a mass of metal work, anchors, chains and rails. Standing upright was a rectangular structure which I took to be the wheelhouse from a motorboat.

Andersen moved up to the corner of the shed and peered around the corner. Then my blood froze as the deep bark of a dog pierced the still night air. Then a low growl and another bark which echoed and clattered around the valley. I scuttled backwards into the shadow of the wheelhouse. Andersen dropped down and lay dead flat on the ground. Both of us were motionless, but the barking continued. I was petrified, my body was rooted to the spot.

The barking came from the direction of the cottages, I heard the creak of a door as it opened and a thin sliver of yellow light appeared. The barking came again, louder this time then a muffled voice. The door slammed and the light disappeared, there was a scuffling and I realised with horror that the dog had been released and was running towards us. I still had a chance to escape, the machine gun was in my hands and I might not be seen in the shadows, but Andersen was still out in the open and totally exposed. My heart pounded wildly as I readied myself for whatever was about to appear.

Then quite unexpectedly, Andersen rose to his knees and stood up. At the same time a black border collie came flying around the corner. It stopped about ten feet away from Andersen, stiffened its front legs and barked viciously at the intruder. Andersen raised his hands and stood dead still. The collie ran back and forth excitedly. Then I heard slow plodding footsteps crunching on the gravel and the dog started to whimper. I dug the butt of the machine gun into my shoulder and raised the barrel as the shadowy figure of a man came into the moonlight. I couldn't see his face, but he didn't look like a soldier and didn't appear to be carrying a weapon. In a low murmur Andersen muttered something in Norwegian and I heard the man reply. The collie now ran around the two men as though it was herding them in from a field. Andersen reached down and gently stroked its head. There were more words in Norwegian and then Andersen turned towards me.

"It's okay, you can come out." I stood up and carefully stepped out of the shadow. I could see that the Norwegian was an older man with a thick grey beard. He wore a heavy jacket and woollen hat. His dark eyes watched me suspiciously.

"This is Fredrik, he will help us," explained Andersen. "He owns the boat yard here and is no friend of the Germans." And then in whispered English, "Keep the gun handy just in case."

Andersen turned to Fredrik and effortlessly slipped back into their Norwegian conversation. I watched on trying to read their body language, but the elderly sailor gave little away. Whatever Andersen had asked for appeared to be accepted, as after some head scratching and a few shoulder shrugs the two men reached out and shook hands.

"He's going to find us some tools," explained Andersen.

In single file we followed Fredrik down the side of the shed to a narrow wooden door. He twisted the handle and with a thrust from his shoulder the door opened. Inside was pitch black. Andersen took the torch from me and switched it on. We followed Fredrik as he bowed his head and stepped inside. The beam of the torch swung around the building. It was a large space cluttered with all manner of maritime equipment. In the centre a large motorboat sat propped up on heavy wooden blocks. Fredrik walked over to a wooden chest which sat on top of a workbench. Andersen shone the torch towards him and cast his face into a sinister shadow. Fredrik flicked open the catches on the chest, lifted the lid and then beckoned Andersen over to look inside. Behind me the door began to swing shut. I stepped back and jammed the heel of my boot against it. I didn't like the idea of being trapped in the shed. Andersen leant over the chest and took out a metal hacksaw, he examined it in the torch light and then handed it to me.

"Take that will you." It wasn't the best of tools for the job, but I guessed that with some persuasion it could cut through the wires. Then Andersen picked up a long handled axe which lay on the bench. This seemed to upset Fredrik and there was another exchange of foreign words. Andersen looked towards me.

"He's saying these tools are expensive and he's worried he won't get them back."

"Can't we leave them somewhere for him when we've finished?" I suggested.

"Not really," Andersen sucked in through his teeth. "Have you got anything we can offer him?" I thought for a moment and stupidly patted my pocket as if I was looking for my wallet, but that was back at Wick and anyhow it was empty. I had the machine gun, but there was no way I'd give that up. The only item of value I had on me was my watch. Reluctantly I pushed the sleeve of my woollen jumper back and revealed the timepiece.

"Yes perfect, that'll do," Andersen spoke without hesitation. "Take it off and give it to him."

He took the hacksaw from me while I undid the leather strap and slid the watch off. I took one last look at the face as it lay in the palm of my hand and wondered if I'd ever own such an expensive piece of jewellery ever again. I passed it over to Fredrik who took it with his wiry hand and brought it up close to his face. He examined it with interest as the torchlight sparkled off the chrome surround and flickered in his eye. He looked at Andersen and gave a craggy smile.

"He's happy," said Andersen with a note of relief.

"I'm not surprised, he's getting one hell of a bargain."

"If it gets you home it's a cheap deal."

As Fredrik handed over the axe the collie, which had been prowling about us, stopped dead still and pricked up his ears. I looked down towards the dog and then back up towards Andersen.

"We've got to get back quickly," he said gravely. "Fredrik says that they heard us land. Apparently there is a German policeman in the village and the chances are he has already sent word to the army garrison in the next valley. They could already be on their way here." A surge of adrenaline took hold of me and I made for the door.

"Wait," said Andersen sternly as he put out his open hand to stop me. "I'll lead the way." With that he murmured a word of thanks to Fredrik and turned to go. Carefully he looked round the open door and satisfied himself that the area was clear before beckoning me on.

Outside we slowly crept to the back of the building and leaving Fredrik behind we started to retrace our steps. I was now desperate to get back to the aircraft and wanted to run as fast as I could, but over the open ground Andersen was rightfully cautious and instead we slowly edged our way up towards the tree line. Then once in the cover of the woods it was a different matter, he moved quickly, almost sprinting. In his right hand he held the handle of the axe, in his left the hacksaw. Caught in the moonlight he looked like a Viking raider charging towards Valhalla. I followed as best I could, darting between the trees and over the uneven ground. It didn't take long before my legs were tired and my lungs were burning, but I ran on knowing we had to get back as soon as we could. In my exertion I quickly became disoriented, all I could do was to chase Andersen in the blind hope that he knew where we had left the dinghy. He veered to the right and picked up a narrow path which ran along the water's edge. Try as I may it was impossible for me to match his long strides and he was now a fair distance in front of me. By the time I'd caught up with him, he had already reached the dinghy and was dragging it towards the water. I stopped, took a deep breath and then, as if possessed by some evil spirit, bent double and vomited.

"Come on, we can't stop," he called back. I composed myself then took hold of the rope. We floated the dinghy a little way out into the fjord and then, being careful not to puncture the rubber, placed the tools in the middle. I stumbled in while Andersen pushed off from the shallows. We paddled out until we were well clear of the bank.

I looked up and saw the Catalina ahead of us. It was a great comfort to see her sat there on the water. I was desperate to be back on board with those engines running, although I knew we still had a lot of work to do in freeing the wingtip.

"We'd better be careful," whispered Andersen. "Just in case something has gone wrong and we're rowing into a trap." I picked up the torch and pointing it towards the stranded aircraft I signalled the three short and three long flashes to Harvey. Almost immediately the Aldis lamp flickered back from the port blister.

"He's seen us,"

"Okay, let's go."

We paddled as quickly as we could, trying not to make too much noise. Through the darkness I could see Harvey's pale face leaning out of the window and smiling towards us. As we got near he reached out and grabbed the side of the dinghy.

"Take these," Andersen handed him the tools.

"Brilliant, that will do the trick," Harvey squawked excitedly when he saw the hacksaw. I took a loose loop of thin rope and secured the dinghy to the side of the aircraft, then pulled myself through the open window and climbed back inside the fuselage. Murphy was crouching by Smithy's bunk in the second compartment.

"Did you have any trouble?" he asked.

"Not really, we managed to get the tools from a friendly villager."

"It felt like you were gone for hours," said Harvey.

I went to look at my watch, but with a sigh of regret remembered I didn't have it anymore. I moved forward so Andersen could heave himself into the aircraft.

"We need to move fast," I spoke urgently at Harvey. Taking the tools, both of us headed up into the cockpit and climbed out between the engines. Carefully we crawled back out along the wing to where the wire cable was embedded in the leading edge.

"Let's hope this works," Harvey muttered as he handed me the hacksaw. "For God's sake don't break the blade!"

I placed my left hand on the wire, it was still under tension. Then with my right hand I began to saw. The wire was made from strong steel and I had made quite an effort before I could see any progress. Then one by one the thin strands began to sever. Halfway through there was a crack.

"Don't get too close," I whispered to Harvey who was craning over me and watching the wire. I carried on sawing, my arm muscles were almost exhausted and my brow was running with sweat. Then suddenly the final strands gave way with a snap and the wire whipped its way over the wing like a startled snake. Below us there came a loud crunch as the debris which had been held by the cable smashed down on the deck of the boat. Harvey laid down and looked over the edge of the wing.

"The wire's free from both sides, it's just the rope that's holding us." I moved forward and with much less effort managed to sever the rope.

"That's it, we should be free."

"Hold on, the float's still caught up," said Harvey who was staring over the edge. I crawled further forward and leant over towards him. He shone the torch down onto the deck of the boat. We had been so distracted by the cable and rope we hadn't seen that the front of the float was snagged under the wooden taffrail.

"Here hold this and pass me the axe when I get down there." Harvey handed me the torch and then swung his body over the wing and jumped down onto the deck of the boat. I reached over as far as I could and then handed down the axe. He steadied himself, adjusted his foot position and then using all his might he raised the axe above his head and brought it down hard on the taffrail. There was a great thud and the head drove itself halfway through the thick wood. Harvey wriggled the axe free and repeated the movement, another great thud and the rail split in two. With a fierce kick he cleared away the rest of the rail and the float freed itself from the boat. I felt the whole aircraft move as it settled back into the water.

"Yes!" I cried in triumph. As I did so, the wing drifted away from the boat. Harvey leapt up to stop it moving away from him, but his reach fell short. I lay there helplessly and for a moment was seized by the fear that after all his efforts Harvey would be left stranded on the boat.

"You're going to have to swim for it!" I called across. It was only a matter of feet, but Harvey looked anxiously at the ice cold water.

"Hold on!" Andersen bellowed from the blister. He swung his legs out, launched himself into the dinghy and then paddled over to rescue the stranded navigator. I crawled back across the wing and dropped down into the cockpit. By the time I got back into the rear compartment, Merrill was helping Harvey and Andersen in through the blister.

"What should we do with the dinghy?" Harvey asked.

"Let the bloody thing go," suggested Merrill.

"No," said Andersen. "Puncture it and bring it inside. It's best we don't leave any clues as to who was here." It took several vicious stabs with Harvey's small pocketknife to deflate the dinghy. Pulling it on board was a struggle, but eventually we had the yellow mass of rubber and canvas stuffed into the tail compartment. I turned to see Murphy standing in the walkway next to the navigation table.

"Is everyone back on board?" he asked.

"Yes, we're good to go skipper," shouted Merrill as he

pushed passed me and climbed up into his seat ready to start the engines. I watched as Murphy turned back into the cockpit and saw something that really disturbed me. Outside the sky was no longer pitch black, the sun was beginning to rise. By the time I'd reached the cockpit Murphy was already flicking the magneto switches. Hearing those great engines burst into life again filled my heart with hope, we had another chance to escape.

"Right, let's try this again," Murphy grabbed the throttles above his head. Before I'd got back into my seat we were already running down the fjord with the water buffeting hard against the fuselage. This time I managed to secure my straps and then readied myself to take the throttles. Over the windscreen the spray obscured our view and I worried we might hit another object, but as we accelerated the view became clearer and I could now see our path was clear. Then with a bump, the metal hull unstuck from the water and we were airborne. I took control of the throttles and Murphy pulled hard back on the yoke. It was a huge comfort to be flying once more, but the landscape below us was all clearly visible now. In daylight we would be a very easy target for even the slowest of enemy fighters.

# Chapter 17

## We've got company

"Head due south for nineteen minutes." Harvey called up into the cockpit. Murphy looked at his watch and then turned the aircraft onto the bearing. We were climbing on full power over the mouth of the fjord. To the east a line of vivid purple light was seeping up from the horizon, it wouldn't be long before the sun followed. As we banked Harvey pointed out of the window.

"Blimey, look at that!" he shouted. Murphy looked down and I craned my neck over the instrument panel to see what he had spotted. The calm water below us had been divided by the wide v shaped bow wave of a boat. At the head was a sleek grey vessel travelling fast towards the fjord.

"It's an E-Boat," exclaimed Murphy. The metal hulled E-Boats were fast patrol craft armed with torpedoes and heavy machine guns. We'd been very lucky, she had obviously been deployed to find us. If we had been delayed any further they would have caught us on the water and no doubt would have made short work of us.

"Christ, that was close," muttered Murphy.

"She's turning," shouted Harvey as the E-boat spun

around in a wide arc leaving a neat trail of disturbed water. "Is she going to fire on us?"

"They can try, but we're too high and fast now. What's more concerning is we've been spotted." Murphy looked up at the sky and squinted. "The quicker we can get out to sea the better."

I rubbed my eyes with both hands and felt how exhausted I was. An odd numbness overcame me and I felt my limbs start to shiver. It was a familiar feeling, I'd felt like this several times after combat, but those dogfights had been short bursts of action. Never before had I experienced such long physical and mental exertion.

"Here, fancy a drink?" It was Harvey again offering me an enamel mug. I perked up immediately thinking he was offering an alcoholic reward, but it was just a mug of water. Nevertheless, I took it gratefully.

Twenty minutes later we were out over the Skagerrak strait and turning southwest. The most dangerous part of our journey was now ahead of us. We would have to pass between the top of Denmark and the southern most part of Norway. Unlike my Spitfire the Catalina couldn't climb very high to avoid trouble. Our only option was to fly down the middle of the straits and hope for the best. In the dark we could have easily slipped by undetected but in daylight it was a different matter. At the narrowest point we would only be thirty-five miles from the fighter station at Kristiansand.

"If you don't mind, I'll get you and Merrill to man the Browning machine guns," Murphy asked. I unstrapped myself and climbed down from the cockpit. Harvey was busy at his table plotting our course. In the compartment behind, Andersen sat upright on a bunk. He looked at me pensively.

"How's it going?"

"We're making good progress." I gave a faint smile and tried to hide my concern. Smithy was still laying on the bunk. In the brighter light I could now see how severe the injury to his head was. His right eye had swollen into a red mass and the dressing that had been applied to his face was soaked in blood. He turned towards me.

"We're on our way home now," I said cheerfully. "Won't be long." Smithy gave no reply.

I reached the rear compartment, took up position in the starboard blister and plugged the headset into the intercom. The field of view was remarkable, I could see the grey sea beneath, the white sky above and the shadow of the coast in the far distance. If we weren't flying through hostile skies it would have been a terrific position to relax and take in the view. Merrill came up and took position in the opposite blister.

"You know how to use that thing?" he pointed to the Browning. I looked at the large machine gun with its thick black barrel and bright brass ammunition hanging from the breech.

"Er, not really," I admitted.

"Make sure it's cocked." He gestured to the bolt that protruded from the side. "And to fire, push the trigger there." Between the two wooden handles was a small metal button which could be operated by the thumb.

"We're in position, skipper," Merrill spoke over the

intercom.

"Okay, keep a bloody good look out."

Once again I felt out of control. Although I wasn't flying, while I was in the cockpit I could see our height, speed and the direction we were heading. Back there in the blister I was devoid of all this information and it made me nervous. I knew we had to fly this course for the best part of an hour, but I had no watch to check the time. All I could do was to make myself as comfortable as I could and watch the world pass by.

It was difficult to stay alert, each one of my limbs ached and the gash on my forehead was now starting to throb. Even with the incessant drone of the radial engines and the wind that whistled through gaps in the windows, I found my eyelids closing. To keep awake, every few minutes I would stand and change position. After a while I noticed Merrill doing the same. Eventually I heard Harvey speak to Murphy over the intercom.

"Five minutes until change of course, Skipper." The message was a great relief, we were almost clear of danger and not a moment too soon as it was now broad daylight. Then something caught my eye.

"Shit!" I shouted aloud.

"What's up?" Merrill looked over with startled concern.

"We've got company." I was staring at a small black dot in the far distance. Merrill leant over my shoulder and peered through the window.

"You sure? I can't see anything?"

"Yes," I called back sharply. With my eyes fixed on the dot I spoke into the intercom. "Skipper, we've got an aircraft on our three o'clock. It's higher than us and about sixteen hundred yards away." I watched as the little dot moved across the sky. "It's a fighter, probably a 109."

"What the hell do we do?" asked Murphy with a note of panic in his voice. There wasn't much that we could do.

"Stay straight and level there's a chance he may not have seen us." But for all my optimism I saw the aircraft was turning and starting to run in towards us.

"He's coming at us," I spoke as calmly as I could.

"I can't see him," Murphy shouted down the intercom. I realised that from his position on the left hand side of the cockpit his view would be obscured.

"He's still there. You'll have to rely on my instructions," I said firmly. "Wait until I shout and then corkscrew to starboard." The corkscrew manoeuvre was a diving turn and about the only evasive action a big aircraft like the Catalina could perform.

"I still can't see him."

"You have to trust me!" I retorted. I reached over the breech and pulled the cocking handle of the Browning back, the bolt flew forward with a heavy clunk as I let go. I squatted down behind the machine gun and swung the barrel to face the oncoming fighter. It was still a fair distance away but closing fast. The chances of me hitting the fighter were very slim, but I had to try. I slipped my thumbs onto the trigger and squeezed. There was an almighty clatter as the gun fired. The noise within the fuselage was ear splitting. The recoil caught me unawares. I struggled to control the weapon and let go of the trigger. The fighter was still flying directly towards us, my short burst of fire had done nothing to dissuade him.

"Get ready, he's nearly on us." We needed to move at exactly the right time, too early and he would follow us down, too late and he would hit us. I let go of the machine gun and steadied myself against the fuselage. The fighter was now very close, I could see it was definitely a 109 with its square wingtips and angular canopy. As I watched two yellow flashes flashed from the guns mounted in his wings. At the same time I heard a metallic thwack to my left.

"Corkscrew now!" I yelled. In one violent movement Murphy pitched the nose of the Catalina down. Merrill slipped from his position and smashed into my side, I grabbed his arm and held him firm. Everything that wasn't fastened slid forward with a crash, a metal ammunition box flew up and smashed the Perspex on the starboard window. I found myself wrestling with the fabric of the dinghy which had come loose from behind. Then like a roller coaster Murphy brought the nose back up and we were level again. I scrambled over Merrill's prostrate body and reached the window just in time to see the 109 heading away from us on the port beam. He was starting to turn and I knew he would be coming in for another attack, this time from the rear.

"Where is he?" came Murphy's impatient voice.

"Off our port, he'll be coming around again."

It suddenly occurred to me that this had been a rash move by the fighter. If he had waited to get on to our rear in the first place, he would have had a better chance of hitting us. Why then would he have tried to attack us as soon as he'd seen us? Maybe he had been looking for us for some time and was now low on fuel? In which case he would want to destroy us as quickly as possible and get home.

"I reckon this guy is low on fuel," I said over the intercom.

"We're a hundred miles out from Kristiansand, so he could be on the extent of his range," Harvey confirmed my suspicion.

"We'll never outrun him, but if we can mess him around for long enough he might have to turn back," I suggested.

"I'm going to try and head for a bank of cloud ahead of us. It's a long shot, but our only chance," said Murphy. I contemplated our situation. Although we couldn't match the fighter for speed we would be able to fly slower than he could. In a three hundred mile an hour aircraft it would be difficult to get an accurate bead on a target moving considerably slower. I scrambled back over to the starboard blister, my feet slipping on the spent cartridge cases that were now strewn over the floor. I could just see that the 109 was now coming round on to our rear quarter.

"Skipper, can you throttle back and lose some height," I asked Murphy.

"What? Why?" came his curt and confused response.

"He'll have to dive to attack us then," I explained. "When he's almost on us, pull hard back and stall the aircraft." Murphy didn't reply, but I felt the aircraft start to descend. I watched carefully as the 109 started to follow us down in a dive, I knew he was now picking up more speed than he needed. "Get ready, he's almost on us. …. Pull up now!" I screamed. It was apparent that Murphy had understood my instructions as the nose of the Catalina shot up and we climbed hard. In doing this our speed had rapidly decreased and the 109 shot passed us in a blur. In attempting to keep us in his sights he turned on his back and briefly lost control, he rolled out and climbed away for another attack. Without prompting, Murphy jammed the controls forward and again put the Catalina into a near vertical dive. The cartridge cases rattled along the floor. I slid forward and cracked my knee on something hard. I put my arm out and managed to prevent myself from headbutting the barrel of the Browning. I looked out and saw we were dropping down towards the North Sea at an alarming speed.

"Where is he?" screamed Murphy.

"Right behind and above us," Merrill shouted from the other side.

I twisted my back and looked round to see the 109 once again plunging into a dive. We had one last chance, we were losing height and I wasn't sure he would fall for the same trick, but we had to try.

"Okay, here he comes again." I braced myself against the gun position. "Get ready, pull up ... now!" Murphy pulled the controls back and we shot up again. I caught a brief glimpse of the sea and was shocked to see we could have only been a few hundred feet from the surface. The aircraft rose up and for a few moments seemed to stand still in the air. This time the pilot of the 109 didn't overshoot, but the manoeuvre prevented him from firing on us. He was obviously aware of our altitude and the danger of hitting the water. He abandoned his attack and turned away.

Murphy lowered the nose and I heard the engine note

pick up as he pushed the throttles forward. We were now only two hundred feet above the sea, we had played every card and our only hope was to run as quickly as we could. I watched the 109 as it turned in a wide figure of eight behind us.

"I can't be sure, but it looks like he's given up," I said cautiously.

"Let's hope so," said Murphy. "I'll keep low until we can climb up into the cloud."

I flexed my shoulders, stretched my arms and tried to shake off the tension of the last two minutes. The 109 was no longer visible and it appeared we were out of danger. I turned to see Andersen standing in the doorway of the compartment. I had completely forgotten about him and Smithy. With what we'd been through they must have been thrown around like rag dolls.

"You okay?" I asked. Without replying he slipped back into the compartment. I took off my headset and followed him. The first thing I noticed was four beams of daylight that streamed into the compartment from a neat line of bullet holes. I remembered the metallic twangs I heard when the 109 opened fire on us. Then I saw him, Smithy the young radio operator, lying motionless on the bunk, his tunic open and his chest ripped apart. His limp hand hung over the side as if he was pointing down. Underneath the bunk a large pool of bright red blood had collected within the ribs of the aluminium floor. Instinctively I turned my head from the awful sight and felt myself wretch.

"I'm sorry. I did everything I could." The sleeves of Andersen's jumper were soaked in blood.

"Are you hurt?" I asked.

"No," he shook his head. I heard a whimper behind me. Merrill had come into the compartment and seen his crew mate lying on the bunk.

"Is he …?"

"Yes, I'm afraid so," said Andersen.

"We're not clear of danger yet." I interrupted them. "You need to man the guns still." Merrill didn't resist, he turned quickly away as, if like me, he couldn't cope with the sight of what he'd just seen.

"You better let the Skipper know." I called after him as he took up his position and plugged his headset back in.

There was already an awful smell in the compartment. A mixture of sweat, blood and fear.

"We'd better cover him up," suggested Andersen. I took a deep breath and somehow managed to pluck up the courage to deal with the body. Without speaking to each other we stripped the other bunks of blankets and with as much dignity as we could, laid them over the corpse. Andersen reached down and tucked the lifeless arm under the covers. Smithy's skin seemed so young and supple compared to Andersen's gnarled and calloused hands.

"I'll help keep a look out," Andersen climbed out into the rear compartment. I had the feeling he didn't want to stay next to the body. I went forward towards the cockpit. Harvey was still at his table, he looked up with a sorrowful expression. I passed through and climbed up into my seat. Murphy gave me a brief nod. He waited until I'd fastened my straps and plugged in my headset, then spoke into the intercom.

"Pay attention everyone," his voice came through clearly. "We've still got a long flight ahead of us and I need everyone to keep their wits about them. There's still a chance a fighter might get at us." His voice had lowered, he appeared to be back in control and had regained his authority. I was glad of that. "Harvey what's our position?"

"We're heading south, I suggest we turn on to bearing two-three-zero. We should make landfall in about three hours."

"Right, bearing two-three-zero," repeated Murphy. He banked the aircraft around to starboard. I watched the compass dial rotate until we were on the new course. By sheer coincidence we were flying the exact same route that I had taken when the engine on my Spitfire had started to misfire.

"That's good skipper, bearing two-three-zero will take us home," said Harvey. I looked ahead. There was nothing to recognise in the white sky above or the grey sea below, but somehow I knew I'd been there before.

We pushed on over the featureless seascape for a good two hours. We were now well out of danger, but there was always the slim possibility that something might go wrong. My biggest fear was that a friendly fighter might confuse us for the enemy.

"Can you take her for a moment," asked Murphy.

"Yes, by all means." I reached forward to take control of the yoke and slid my feet on to the rudder bar.

"You have control," said Murphy.

"I have control," I confirmed.

He let go of the yoke and then stretched his arms out

with an elongated yawn. He unbuckled the straps and climbed down from the seat. He spent a good ten minutes talking to the others in the back and checking on the damage. While he was gone I kept the Catalina on course and monitored the engines. It took a lot of concentration and I was glad of the distraction. Strangely Murphy would never have given me the controls for so long on the way over, but then a lot had happened in the last six hours.

When he came back up I felt his hand on my left shoulder. I turned and he smiled.

"You're doing well." There was still a note of condescension in his tone. "We'll make a sailor of you yet!" he joked with a grin.

# Chapter 18

## Bound by the official secrets act

"We're about twenty minutes out Skipper, you should see the coastline soon," said Harvey over the intercom.

"Righto. Thanks Nav," replied Murphy. It was now eight o'clock, we were four and a half hours overdue.

"Running a bit hot on the port," said Merrill who had now taken up his position monitoring the engines. "She should be okay, but I suggest we reduce the revs." Murphy raised his hand and brought the throttle back slightly.

Then in front of us, just below a band of mist, I saw the coastline.

"There's Scotland!" I shouted jubilantly. Harvey appeared between our shoulders.

"What a sight," he murmured emotionally. We had been through a horrendous ordeal and the relief of seeing the Caledonian coastline almost brought me to tears.

"This bearing should bring us right over the airfield." He was correct, ten minutes later we passed over the wreck of the steam launch on the beach and there below was the wide concrete runway. The cloud was low and the area was shrouded in a misty drizzle. We flew straight over the top of the airfield at five hundred feet and then took a wide circuit around the perimeter.

"I think they know we're coming in," said Murphy as he pushed forward and we started to descend into the final approach.

"Don't forget the undercarriage," I reminded him with an impertinent smile.

"I won't!" he glared back at me. With an amphibious aircraft it was difficult to remember when to put the wheels down or keep them up. Murphy twisted the lever and I heard the whine of the hydraulics as the wheels lowered. He banked the wing and brought the aircraft round to line up directly with the runway and throttled back.

Landing in the Catalina was much more pleasant than landing in a Spitfire. There was an unrestricted view over the nose and you could come in slower without fear of stalling. The wide undercarriage and big tyres were also more stable and forgiving.

The main wheels touched down and almost a second later the nose wheel lowered onto the concrete. Murphy used the full length of the runway to slow the aircraft down gently. At the very end he applied the port brake and we turned up towards the watch tower. I could see several erks already waiting for us by one of the trucks. There were also two figures watching us from the corner of the tower. The Station Commander in his Macintosh and Collings clearly unphased by the miserable weather, in his naval uniform.

With a burst of power Murphy turned the Catalina around to face the oncoming wind and then one at a time shut down the engines. The whole aircraft appeared to sag with relief as did my body. Immediately the erks ran forward to chock the wheels and make the aircraft safe.

Murphy unbuckled his seat straps and I followed him down into the back of the aircraft. We squeezed passed Harvey who was packing up his charts and instruments.

"Don't forget to burn that lot," Murphy reminded him.

The rear of the aircraft was an awful mess. Anything that had not been tied down was lying on the floor. We picked our way carefully through the debris. As if to pay his respects Murphy stopped briefly and looked at the blanket covering Smithy's body. The pool of blood under the bunk had spread out and congealed into a dark red stain.

There was a clunk in the next compartment and I saw that Merrill was lowering the access ladder through the broken starboard blister. One of the erks, a man with a round freckled-face, appeared at the window.

"We need a stretcher," Andersen said to him.

"And an ambulance," added Murphy.

"Yes sir." The man disappeared back down the ladder.

A few minutes later a light blue Austin lorry with a red cross painted on the side drew up alongside. There were some hurried words and a canvas stretcher was passed up through the window and laid down across the walkway.

"Do you need a hand there?" asked the freckle-faced man through the window.

"No thank you, we will bring him out," said Murphy with a solemn sense of duty. He moved back to the bunk and placed his arms under Smithy's shoulders, Andersen stepped forward and took hold of his legs. Together they lifted the rigid body from the bunk and carefully moved it through the compartment and onto the stretcher. As they did so the blanket slipped and revealed his face, Harvey looked away. I pulled the blanket back up and helped to steady the stretcher. With some difficulty we passed Smithy's body out through the window. Two men on the other side carried him down the ladder and into the ambulance. Murphy leant against the window and watched as the men secured the stretcher and shut the ambulance doors. Andersen stooped down and picked up the important backpack.

"Thank you gentlemen," he reached out and shook hands with each one of us. "I'm truly grateful for your help. You may never know how important last night's operation was." He looked at me. "Thank you for giving up your watch. I hope it wasn't expensive." I laughed and shook my head. I had no idea of its value apart from the fact that I knew I couldn't afford to replace it. Outside the ambulance started its engine and pulled away. "I'm very sorry about your crew mate. I wish I could have done more to help." He turned to the window. "I'm afraid I have to get going." He swung his legs through the opening and climbed out.

Collings was waiting for Andersen at the foot of the ladder. He appeared to know the secret agent well as he met him with a large smile and friendly slap on the shoulder.

I was beginning to find the atmosphere inside the aircraft claustrophobic and now we were on the ground I was keen to get out. I followed Murphy and climbed down the ladder; even in the miserable wet weather it felt good to have my feet back on British soil. Merrill came next. I helped him find his footing as his legs were shaking badly.

He was followed by Harvey holding his map case, stuffed with charts.

"That's a strange looking bird." I spun round to see Merrill pointing to a civilian aircraft parked on the far side of the watch tower. It was a sleek looking machine, silver in colour with two engines. Standing at the rear by the open door were two men, both wearing long black overcoats. The four of us stood watching as Andersen and Collings walked over towards them. They greeted each other and Andersen handed his backpack to one of them. Then Andersen and the two men boarded the aircraft leaving Collings outside. He shut the door for them and then stood back.

"I wonder what it was all about?" asked Harvey as the engines of the silver aircraft started.

"No idea," said Merrill. "But that bag was filled with some kind of liquid in metal cannisters." We all looked at him in surprise. "Well, while you went looking for those tools curiosity got the better of me, I had to have a look," he explained. "I reckon it's some top-secret fuel." Murphy laughed and slapped him on the back.

"Remind me never to leave my luggage with you."

The aircraft moved on to the airfield, Collings turned away and with a purposeful stride walked back towards us.

"I gather you've had quite an exciting night," he said cheerfully. "We were wondering where on earth you'd got to. There's food inside and the kettle's on." He nodded towards the watch tower. "I'm afraid, we've still got some work to do. I need a full report from all of you."

The room we had been briefed in had been locked when

we departed and everything was as we left it twelve hours before. The photographs and charts were still scattered over the table, the ashtrays were full and our mugs were collected in the middle. Strangely it felt like the mess had been made by someone else, like the morning after a party we hadn't been invited to. We threw our belongings down and slouched into the chairs. There was one empty seat at the end. On the table Smithy's playing cards lay in a half finished game of solitaire.

Collings followed us in, bringing with him the officer with the revolver and an admin clerk who carried a portable typewriter. Between us we gave a detailed report of the operation. Collings wanted to know everything and I had to give my account of what happened when we went on the search for tools. His questions were relentless: what time did we leave the aircraft? How far did we go? Describe the Norwegian you met? While we spoke, the officer took notes and the clerk bashed away at the typewriter. Eventually Collings seemed content that we had told him all we knew.

"I think we can safely say the operation was a success," Collings said as we devoured the bacon and eggs that had been brought in for us. "I don't think I need to remind you that you're all bound by the Official Secrets Act and under no circumstances are you allowed to discuss any details of the operation with anyone else." He stood up and started to pack his papers away. "You're no longer required by me, so all of you are to report back to your respective units." The clerk opened the door and flooded the room with bright sunlight. "Goodbye and good luck gentlemen." He turned and headed out into the corridor.

"If we're not needed I'm going to get my head down." I announced as I lit a cigarette.

"Don't blame you, it sounds like a good idea," agreed Murphy.

I stood up and gathered my flying gear together.

"I'll see you in the bar later?" I asked Murphy, he nodded back and as I walked past he grabbed my arm.

"I reckon if you hadn't been with us that 109 would have chewed us up and spat us out. Thanks." I was stunned by his compliment and gave him an embarrassed smile in response. He looked up at my forehead. "I'd get that cut seen to, it looks nasty."

I left the room and taking his advice walked over to the medical office. It was a warm spring morning. A bright red tractor was slowly plodding along the side of the runway and sending the sweet scent of cut grass into the air.

"That's a real shiner," said the doctor examining the cut. "I'll get the nurse to clean it up and put a dressing on." He took a box of pills from the medicine cabinet. "If you start to get a headache take two of these. They are quite strong so don't drink alcohol with them." I frowned at his advice. "I'll sign you off for a few days as well."

"Sorry, what do you mean?"

"You can't fly with a head injury like that."

"Is it that bad?"

"No not really, but I can't take the chance that you might start fainting or seeing double." He took a pad of forms from his desk and started to scribble down notes on my condition. "I want to see you in two days, if it's looking better you can get airborne again."

He sent me into the next room where an elderly nurse tended the wound. Eventually, after prodding the bruise and stinging my eye with surgical spirit she declared I was fit to leave.

It was nearly midday when I walked back over to the mess. I was hungry and looking forward to a drink in the bar. There was a clattering in the distance and I heard an aircraft start its engines. A young erk passed me and saluted, I returned the salute with difficulty as the dressing on my forehead was in the way. As I reached the steps that led up to the officer's mess I looked back to see the aircraft heading down the runway and lifting off into the cloud scattered sky. To my amazement, I saw it was the Catalina. I watched it climb and then turn out towards the west. Obviously Murphy and his crew were heading home. As the noise of the engines faded away I was left feeling abandoned. I'd only been with them for a very short time, but I felt that I'd become part of that crew. I turned away with a pang of disappointment.

In my room I took off my jumper and discovered a large hole in the side. At some point during the night's adventure I must have snagged it on something. I undid my boots and on my trouser leg found a dark stain. With a shudder I remembered the pool of blood under Smithy's bunk. In my pocket I was surprised to find a spent cartridge from one of the Brownings. In all the confusion it must have flicked up and caught in my clothing. I turned the cylindrical brass case between my fingers then placed it upright on the bedside table. I threw my clothes into the corner of the room and then lay on the bed.

It was late afternoon when I woke. I took a shallow bath, shaved and changed. I washed my face as best I could, but the area around the wound was very tender. Looking as respectable as I could make myself I headed down to the dining room. Lamont spotted me sitting alone and came over.

"What the hell happened to you?" He winced at the dressing on my forehead.

"In short, I was going down and the instrument panel was coming up, we met in the middle."

"Blimey, looks painful. We got the message that you're off games for the next two days." He sat down in the chair opposite. "You know old Prowse went bloody mad, he thought you'd buggered off on your own somewhere."

"Really?" I grinned at the thought of the intelligence officer panicking over my absence.

"Yes, he was all for getting an arrest warrant drawn up for you. It was only when the Station Commander got on the phone did he calm down." Lamont poured himself a glass of water from the jug on the table. "Kalman says he saw you climbing out of that Catalina this morning. Is that true?" I didn't answer. "Come on, spill the beans, what did you get up to?" It was then I felt the difficult situation I was in. I couldn't tell him anything about the operation and this was unusual for me. Even after the toughest of dogfights I'd had the opportunity to talk to friends and comrades about what I'd been through. The night before had been a hellish experience mentally, physically and emotionally and I had no release. I realised then that I needed to bury those memories deep down inside.

"Oh, it was only a navigation thing they wanted help with, a short trip out over Shetland and back." I lied.

Later we moved into the lounge and claimed a pair of stools by the bar.

"Kalman was sent off to search for some German battleship this afternoon," Lamont told me. "Top brass were getting very twitchy about something."

"Did he find it?"

"No, so I'm scheduled to go looking for it tomorrow." He looked at his watch. "It's a first light take off, so I'm going to get my head down." He slid off the stool and downed the last of his drink.

Left alone in the bar I started to wonder if I could ever prove that I had been to Norway. Apart from the brass cartridge case on my bedside table I had no evidence. Murphy and the Catalina had flown off, so had Andersen and his backpack. In fact, the more I thought about it the more I wondered if it ever had happened at all. I ordered another drink and tried to shake the feeling off, but I had no luck.

# Chapter 19

## Heading south

The following morning all hell broke loose in the PR unit. The German battleship Bismarck was rumoured to be moving around the fjords and everyone, except me, was out looking for it. Although I felt fit to fly I was firmly grounded.

It was hugely frustrating to know that Lamont and Kalman were hunting the grand prize. To reduce the distance to Norway and extend their flight time, both had moved their aircraft up to Sumburgh on Shetland.

I spent the morning in the crew room, thumbing my way through my book and dozing in-between cigarettes. At lunchtime Jenny was given a twenty minute break from the interpretation room so I joined her on the grass outside the huts.

"What on earth happened to your head?" she asked with concern.

"I was fighting for the dignity of an innocent maiden," I quipped.

"Um really?" She screwed up her face sarcastically. "I hope the other chap came off worse." It was warm, I'd taken off my tunic and was sitting in my shirt sleeves.

"How's the Lobster this morning?"

"Frantically pacing up and down the office like an expectant father." She looked out across the airfield. "I suppose we can only wait." My eye wandered down her body and came to rest on her slender legs.

"How long before you're flying again?" I looked up and found she was staring at me. "I'm worried that you'll become a nuisance if you're left on the ground too long."

"Doc says two days, if it's healed up." I touched the dressing. "I hope it doesn't leave a scar."

"Might make you look tough and rugged."

"I thought I already looked like that."

"No, I'd say more … youthful and handsome."

"Is that a compliment or just an observation?"

"I'll let you decide." She gave a subtle smile. Behind her, in the far distance I spotted an aircraft.

"Looks like one of the boys." We both watched the aircraft as it circled the airfield and came into land.

"I'd best get back to work." She stood up. "Now, be a gentleman and look the other way while I adjust my skirt."

"Do I have to?"

"Yes." She flicked her hand out and ushered my gaze away.

I watched the Spitfire taxiing up towards us. As it turned I caught sight of the tail number and realised it was neither Kalman nor Lamont's aircraft. Jenny headed back to the interpretation hut and I wandered down towards the Spitfire as its engine shut down and the pilot climbed out. Prowse appeared from his office and drew up alongside me.

"That's your replacement."

"Replacement?" I stopped in my tracks.

"Yes, seeing as you're no use to us they've sent someone up from Benson. By the way, your orders are to head back down there as soon as possible."

Benson was a new airfield in Oxfordshire where the Heston Photo Reconnaissance operation had been moved to.

"How do I get down there?" I asked assuming there would be some form of transport aircraft heading back that way.

"I've got you a rail warrant."

"Rail warrant!" I protested. "It'll take ages by train."

"I dare say it will, but you're not fit to fly and no transport aircraft are available. I'm sure you can get a lift to the station if you ask nicely at the guard room."

I was furious, after what I'd been through I now had the indignity of having to sit on a long train journey. I sighed and consoled myself that at least I'd be getting away from Prowse.

"Well, there's no point in waiting around is there," I snapped and went to march off towards the mess, but a familiar voice stopped me.

"Hello Jack," The pilot of the Spitfire had removed his helmet. it was Chilton.

"Hello," I replied. "What are you doing up here?"

"Not sure yet." He shrugged his shoulders. "I only got the orders this morning."

"Pilot Officer Chilton?" Prowse interrupted our reunion with an officious glare.

"Yes sir," Chilton replied smartly.

"Report over to the crew room now." Chilton hurriedly gathered his parachute and helmet together and walked off towards the hut. I felt sorry for the poor man and silently wished him good luck with the Lobster.

I waited until the two men disappeared into the crew room and then carefully edged my way around the buildings. With Prowse busy briefing Chilton the coast was clear for me to slip into the interpretation hut. Jenny was sitting alone at a map table.

"What are you doing in here?" She looked up with surprise.

"I'm off I'm afraid." I was pleased to see a fleeting hint of sadness cross her face. "My orders are to report to Benson." She put down the pencil she was holding.

"Are you coming back?"

"I'm not sure." The bright sunlight was softly reflecting off the white wall and outlining her delicate jawline. Briefly our eyes met.

"Jenny ... would you marry me?" Her whole face lit up with an outrageous laugh.

"After only one picnic! You'll have to offer more than that."

"Dinner then?"

"When and where?"

"Not sure when, but somewhere expensive."

"Um, I'll think about it." She stood up, stepped towards me and took my arm.

"You promise to keep in touch." I nodded. She reached up and kissed my cheek and in the very corner of her eye, I noticed a tiny tear glisten. I suddenly had an urge to leave. I was desperate for her company, but at the same time the fear of allowing her to get close overcame me. As I walked away I looked back across the room and her expression seemed to echo my feelings. War was not a good time to fall in love.

Back in the mess I packed my kit bag and cleared my room. I picked up the cartridge case and studied my elongated reflection in the shiny brass. I decided to keep it as a good luck charm and tucked it into my pocket.

"I don't suppose you've got a railway timetable anywhere?" I asked the clerk on the reception desk downstairs.

"Actually, we do." he disappeared below the counter and came back up with a dog-eared copy of a Bradshaw's guide. "Where are you heading?"

"Oxfordshire."

"My, that'll be a long journey." He handed over the booklet. "I suggest you head for Inverness and pick up the night sleeper." My heart sank at the thought of being cramped into a packed railway carriage for the next twenty-four hours.

"Oh, by the way a parcel was left for you this morning." He disappeared down behind the counter again, but this time he came back up with a large package wrapped in brown paper. It was badly crumpled with my name scrawled on the top. There was no post mark, so I assumed it had been delivered by hand. A folded piece of notepaper was gummed to the side. I tore it off and read the writing. It appears we may have a mutual friend. All the best Collings.

I placed the note down and carefully undid the package.

"Bugger me!" I exclaimed.

"What is it sir?" asked the clerk with confusion.

"It's my greatcoat." There on the counter folded neatly was the coat I'd lost all those weeks ago in London. I picked the note back up and read it again. A mutual friend? Surely that could only be Fanshaw? I shook my head in disbelief.

The following evening, after a horrendous journey I found myself at Oxford railway station. Although I was tired and hungry I was surprised to find a pleasant comfort in returning to my home county and the familiar surroundings.

It was Monday evening and a deep scrum of people were pushing their way onto the train that I'd just stepped down from. I jammed my body into an alcove next to a broken vending machine and waited for the crowd to disperse. According to the soot covered clock above the platform it was nearly six o'clock. The impatient guards herded people on board and then one by one slammed the doors shut behind them. A shrill whistle was answered with a pipe from the engine and a squirt of steam blew out from the boiler. With the platform cleared I picked up my bag and squeezed through the turnstiles to the pavement outside.

An old black Austin taxi sat waiting for fares, the driver engrossed in a newspaper. I was just about to knock on his window when the honk of a car horn caught my attention. I looked up the road and to my astonishment saw my own Bentley pull up to the curb. Sitting in the driving seat and waving happily at me was Rowbotham.

"We got the message that you were coming in so I thought I'd pop over and pick you up." I threw my kitbag onto the rear seat. "I hope you don't mind, we've been borrowing the car for a bit."

"No, not in the slightest. I'm glad it's been used." I really didn't mind, in fact I had wondered if I'd ever see the car again. I lifted my foot onto the small step and swung myself into the passenger seat. Such was my life now that possessions meant little to me, but the bond between that car and me was greater than some of my personal relationships. It felt good to be sitting on the sagging leather seat with the large dashboard in front and the engine purring smoothly, even if I wasn't driving.

"I'm not sure what you've been told, but we moved the whole PR operation up from Heston about three weeks ago," Rowbotham explained as he pulled away. "Heston had its charm, but we've got better facilities here. It's very modern and it's got a good mess." He drove quickly through the streets and took the main road heading south.

It wasn't long before the city gave way to the sprawling Oxfordshire countryside which was lush in the new growth of late spring. I bowed my head beneath the windscreen and lit a cigarette. Looking up I saw a formation of Spitfires flying high overhead. The three aircraft were silhouetted neatly against the layer of feathery clouds above them. It was a section from a fighter squadron patrolling towards the south.

"Someone's looking for trouble," remarked Rowbotham who had also seen them. I watched until the overhanging trees barred my view.

It was a short drive to Benson through the country lanes. We drove straight through the main gates and up to the large hangars where we parked.

"This is our lot. That's the hangar and the office is over there," said Rowbotham pointing to a single story camouflaged building. "By the way what happened to your forehead?"

"Oh that, just a bump." I was getting tired of explaining myself. We left the car and walked over towards the office. From somewhere behind the hangar, I could hear a gramophone playing 'How deep is the ocean?' over the banging of metal and the hiss of an air compressor. We reached the building and Rowbotham pushed opened the door. Singleton sat at a large desk, half obscured by a familiar sweet smelling cloud of pipe smoke. He watched us enter and grinned.

"How was Scotland dear boy?" He leant forward on the desk with both elbows.

"Interesting and wild," I replied vaguely. Through the window behind him I saw a Spitfire sitting on the edge of the airfield. It was painted pale blue exactly like the aircraft I'd been flying back and forth over the North Sea. The thought of those long monotonous flights filled me with a dreadful depression. I remembered the three fighters we had just seen and strangely found myself longing for the excitement of combat.

"Sir … can I apply for a transfer…?"

# Author's Historical Note

The inspiration for Bearing Two Nine Two came about on a miserable grey afternoon in Hounslow. I was driving out of London on the M4 motorway and stopped at the service station between junction 3 and 2. Service stations always excited me as a child, stopping at one usually meant we were off on a family adventure. These days, I find them more interesting than exciting. If I have the time I'll buy a drink and watch the eclectic mix of characters as they move through the foyer on their search for caffeine, nicotine, food or just simply the toilets.

On this particular day I was squeezing between two parked cars when I noticed a stone tablet fixed to the wall of the main building. It had been erected by the Airfields of Britain Conversation Trust and marked the site of Heston Airfield. I was intrigued, as I'd just read an account of Sidney Cotton, the flamboyant Australian aviator and his photo reconnaissance unit that he established at Heston. With the help of my smartphone, I discovered Heston airfield had closed in 1947 and later the M4 motorway had been built right over the top of the site. I was now standing on one of the old runways. Inside, I ordered a coffee and instead of people watching, I looked out of the window and imagined a little blue Spitfire bouncing down the runway and taking flight just above the lorry park.

Photo reconnaissance is often overlooked in historical accounts of the Second World War and yet the intelligence gathered by these units was vital to the Allied war effort. Almost every military operation, from small scale commando raids to large offensives were planned using the thousands of aerial photographs taken and delivered by RAF PR units.

I'm not sure that many pilots transferred into PRU from fighter squadrons, but I thought that Jack Sommers, with his flying experience and navigation skills, would have made a good PR pilot.

With both books in this series I've constructed a fictitious narrative around actual events, places and technology. At the start of the story we find Sommers flying low over France. In early 1941 Spitfires were operating from RAF Manston in Kent and carrying out offensive sweeps over occupied France. These operations were costly in terms of losses and from some of the accounts I've read not popular with the pilots. Johnny Johnson, the RAF's highest scoring fighter ace, was quite derogatory about 'Rhubarb' operations. In his 1956 book 'Wing Leader' he states 'I loathed those Rhubarbs with a deep, dark hatred. Apart from the flak, the hazards of making a let-down over unknown territory and with no accurate knowledge of the cloud base seemed far too great a risk for the damage we inflicted.'

After voicing his opinion about these operations Sommers is transferred to Heston. On his way he drives through the East End of London, which has been devastated by aerial bombing. Today this area of London has been developed and in some cases redeveloped, but you don't have to look hard to find scars left by the Blitz. A good example of this is the church that Sommers passes in his Bentley, All Hallow's by the Tower. It still stands today as a very active parish church, although it was completely gutted in 1940. If you have the chance to visit you'll noticed how the black and tarnished medieval walls blend into the fresh modern render and new wooden roof.

At Heston, Sommers is equipped with a modified Supermarine Spitfire. The Spitfire is arguably one of the most famous military aircraft ever produced. Although its often considered as a fast and agile fighter, it was also a very successful reconnaissance aircraft, a role it would keep well into the 1950s.

The Spitfire that Sommers would have been flying was a PR Mk IV. For a single engine aircraft it had an enormous range. In fact, on one early PR sortie a Mk IV piloted by Flying Officer Millen flew from England to Stettin on the Baltic Coast and back, a return trip of 1400 miles that took five hours and twenty minutes. It was operations like this that proved how far the RAF could now see into enemy territory.

Heading north to Scotland takes Sommers away from the South of England where he had spent most of the war and his young life. The airfield at Wick still exists today as a regional airport. It was built at the beginning of the war for Coastal Command Maritime Patrols. However, its location on the northwest tip of the country was an ideal base from which to launch PR operations over Norway and Denmark. As a result, Number 1 PRU was established there in 1940.

Norway had been occupied by Nazi Germany in June 1940. The country, with its vast mountain ranges, was rich in minerals that were vital to the Nazi war effort. Over the course of the war, a variety of allied operations were launched into Norway and the need for good quality photo reconnaissance was vital. PR pilots operating from Scotland were kept busy providing these. While writing and researching this section it struck me how these Spitfire PR sorties were unique in terms of airmanship. All other RAF operations were either flown in larger aircraft with a crew, or in a formation alongside other aircraft. Save for the odd fighter patrol, no other pilots flew alone so deep into enemy territory. It must have been very lonely flying high above an unforgiving sea and jagged mountain ranges for hours on end.

Amongst the pilots stationed at Wick was Alastair 'Sandy' Gunn, a Scotsman from Auchterarder. On the 5th of March 1942 he took off to photograph Trondheim harbour but was shot down. He bailed out and subsequently became a prisoner of war in the notorious Stalag Luft III. He was one of the fifty prisoners of war who were executed when they tried to escape in 1944. That story was immortalised in the 1963 film The Great Escape.

The remains of Sandy's Spitfire, which would have been very similar to the type that Sommers flew, lay scattered over the Norwegian countryside for nearly eighty years. In 2018 a team from the UK managed to recover a significant amount of the wreckage and, as I write this, it is currently being restored to fly again.

The arrival of the Catalina and Sommers' adventure to the Solvik Fjord was based on similar operations that took place all over Scandinavia and other occupied parts of

Europe. Along with Catalinas, other types of flying boats were also used for these operations, including a captured German Heinkel 115. This is detailed by John A Iverach in his book 'The Chronicles of a Nervous Navigator'. At one point he describes waiting for a secret agent to approach from the darkness while he holds a Tommy gun in his hands.

I have a personal connection with Catalinas which is tainted with tragedy. In July 1998 I witnessed a Catalina crash and sink on Southampton Water. Both of my parents were on board and although they managed to escape, two of the passengers drowned. The image of the aircraft hitting the water and slewing sideways is etched deep in my memory and often reappears in times of stress.

These days, aerial surveillance has a huge variety of uses, from scientific monitoring to town planning and of course military intelligence. Although most of the work today is carried out by satellites and autonomous aircraft, the concept remains the same as it did eighty years ago. I hope in some way that this book pays tribute to the work of Sidney Cotton and those trail blazing pilots of the Allied Photo Reconnaissance Units that risked their lives to bring back that all important intelligence.

**Andy Jones**
Romsey, Hampshire
May 2025

www.ajonesauthor.com